Die, Damn You, Die!

By

Des Dunn

as

Sheldon B. Cole

First Published by Cleveland Publishing.

Republished in 2026 by Echo Books.

Echo Books is an imprint of Superscript Publishing Pty Ltd.
ABN 76 644 812 395.
Registered Office: 35 Keeley Lane, Princes Hill, Victoria, 3054.
www.echobooks.com.au

Book Design: Jason McGregor.

ISBN: 978-1-923441-34-7 (Paperback)
ISBN: 978-1-922603-43-2 (ePub)

CHAPTER ONE

Not Wanted

From where he stood in the creek washing down Sundown's blue-black coat, Blake Durant could barely see them coming because the evening light was bad, especially along the creek bank down which the five of them walked. He couldn't make out their faces, but during the weeks since the wagon train started rolling he'd seen them many times, so the face of each was engraved in his mind. They were impatient men, hungry for the journey's end and worn out from travelling, and he knew that in the heart of each was the longing to stop. But they couldn't stop, for they were men of vision and in them was the golden promise of distant lands, a future that offered infinitely more than the pasts they had knownand suffered through.

Durant pulled Sundown from the water and quickly wiped him dry. He had him hitched under the trees when the five drew up. Art Schofield was in front, tall and taciturn, with the confident bearing of a wrangler who knew his business. Then came Jute Carney, skinny, slat-like, his features pinched, a sneer glued to the side of his thin, mean mouth; Jimmy Blunt, always smiling, always bidding a fair day or night to somebody, proving himself a friend as if to belie the menace in his double-holstered gunbelt and his face which was scarred from meetings with men who had been far from friendly; Roland Farner, big and burly, with farmer written all over him, a man who seemed to be on his own even when in a crowd; and Rick Trice, who tried futilely to hide the fact that Farner's daughter, Ellen, had him going round in circles.

What Trice was doing there, Blake Durant had no idea. But he knew what was on the minds of the other four.

He said, "You had your meeting, Farner?"

Roland Farner nodded grimly. He seemed for a moment relieved that Durant had addressed him instead of Schofield and his friends.

"Yes, we had a meeting as we said we would, Durant... as we had to have. After all that wrangling last night, something had to be decided upon. The business had to be brought to a head, so to speak."

Blake Durant studied him calmly. What he knew of Farner, he liked. The man was the unchallenged leader of the farmer faction. What he said was listened to and accepted; Farner never had to resort to overbearing manners. It was almost as though what he thought came from the minds of the others.

"What's your decision?" Blake asked.

"Boils down to you shiftin' on, Durant," said Art Schofield roughly. "Pronto!"

Blake saw a deep frown suddenly come to Farner's face. The big farmer took a deep breath and planted his boots wider apart. "I said I'd handle this affair, Schofield," he told the tall wrangler. "I don't want to make this anymore unsavory than it has to be."

"Ain't nothin' unsavory about tellin' a nuisance to git," put in Jute Carney, his lean, lantern-jawed face relieved of its blemishes in the dim light of dusk.

"And the sooner the better," Jimmy Blunt added, rubbing a palm across the butt of his right-hand gun.

Blake Durant ignored their interruption. "What does your decision amount to?" he asked Roland Farner.

Farner worked his mouth, his brow rutted. He was clearly unhappy with the way things were going. Standing off from him, Rick Trice looked slightly nervous, out of his depth in this kind of talk.

"Well, Durant it ain't that we've got anything personal against you. As we see it, you've done everything asked of you since you joined up with us. You've been the best hunter on the wagon train and the best trail scout. If it hadn't been for you, we'd have missed Mintoka Springs and been short of water by now. But you and Stanton ... well, you just don't hit it off and I'm damned if I know why. Stanton's done everything asked of him, too. Everything he said about this trail has turned out to be right. Plenty of feed for the stock, enough water, no mountain passes to negotiate, no real trouble of any kind. It's been pleasant travelling for men and women alike. We have no complaints about Stanton at all, and we intend to follow him right through to the end, to where he says we can stop the wagons and settle."

Blake eyed Schofield, Carney and Blunt carefully before he replied. "My argument with Stanton is based almost completely on my knowledge of what lies ahead of us. I've told all of you many times what that is, a hellion outfit which has made this territory its own. I've seen their tracks and I tell you again there's a dozen men out there, trailing us, watching us. Why they've delayed this long I've no idea, but I feel obliged to repeat my warning: They're waiting for something, maybe for you to tire or get careless."

"How come you're the only one who's seen the tracks of 'em, Durant?" Schofield asked. "Are you sayin' you got the only eyes in these parts that can read trail sign?"

"I seem to have the only pair of eyes looking in the right places, Schofield," Durant returned calmly.

Schofield's lips curled back in a sneer. Carney shifted a little away from Blake, dropping his right shoulder and easing his left hand towards his gun butt. Blake Durant ignored the menace of Carney. His business was with Farner and although he didn't care much which way this discussion went, he felt obligated to put Farner right as best he could. He knew he wasn't a man who made friends easily, but gradually the ice was melting with Farner and his farmer friends. The clannishness had slowly begun to break down and he'd almost reached the point of being accepted unconditionally. He realized it wasn't easy for them to accept him. In their eyes he was a man on the drift, a loner going their way for reasons of his own. They were simple men and they expected others to be the same.

"Listen to me, Farner," Blake went on, looking straight at Farner and no one else. "Even if everything Stanton has promised has come true with respect to the trail, there's nothing for you at the end of it. Colonel Howie owns all the land past the big desert. He has a cattle empire that he's proud of and is determined to keep. I know you've heard the stories, and I know you've also been informed that the good land farther north is there for the taking and there'll be no trouble in getting it. But Stanton insists on taking you along a route where trouble will inevitably come. When the wagons stop rolling, you won't be allowed to settle."

Farner's face grew lines and his lips thinned. He said, "Mike Stanton is of a different belief, Durant, and I'm still inclined to put my trust in him. He says that all the land we're headin' for hasn't been legally claimed. Anyway, what would one man want with all that country? Surely there's space for all, and especially for honest people who ask nothing of anybody and want only to be left alone so they can work for their families and make a new life for themselves."

Blake Durant could offer no further argument. So he shrugged his shoulders and looked west, where the dark hills had the promise of peace and solitude.

Then Rick Trice joined in. "Durant, Mr. Stanton says there's land for all of us out there—good land, with plenty of water. He says that folks like us, keen to work for the future, would have a town built in next to no time. We'd have something for ourselves."

"And what Mike Stanton says is true," Schofield put in sourly. "Anybody who says different is a liar, Durant."

Blake's gaze moved to the tall man. Inwardly he was seething. The wagon train meant nothing to him. Yet he found himself still anxious to argue his case against these men. He didn't understand why. He had his own plans and had a lot of country to travel before he could begin putting them into operation. He needed none of these people. He didn't even know them, and he doubted if any of them liked him. There had been too much evidence of men in the train suspecting him of joining the trek west for reasons that wouldn't be to their advantage.

To Farner he said coolly, "What is it? Do you want me to ride out?"

Farner bit his lip, then nodded gravely. "Yes, Durant. We feel there will be less friction and argument with you gone. I don't think we're doing you an injustice. You don't strike me as being the kind of man who needs the company of others, and you don't appear to be in any way frightened of what might be ahead of you. You came into our midst suddenly and offered no explanation. Now I feel obliged to stand by those I know."

Blake nodded and stepped away. He picked up his saddle and threw it on Sundown. "It's your wagon train," he muttered. "I'll be gone inside of an hour."

"Thank you," said Farner. Then, giving Rick Trice a nod, he turned and walked away.

But, when he'd gone a short distance and the others hadn't followed, Farner wheeled, frowning.

"Mr. Schofield, our business here is finished," he said, and Art Schofield's head came up sharply and his eyes leveled on Farner. Carney and Jimmy Blunt straightened. They wanted Art Schofield to put Farner in his place, Blake thought. But Schofield's tense look faded almost as quickly as it had formed and he said:

"Surely, Mr. Farner, surely. Just stayin' to make sure Durant doesn't pull any tricks."

"I'm positive he won't," Farner said tightly. "Whatever else he has shown himself to be, he certainly hasn't indicated that he isn't a man of his word. I've taken his word, and so will all of us. Now leave him be. Mike Stanton will probably be anxious to know the outcome of our visit; I leave it to you to inform him of it."

Farner stood there in a waiting attitude. Schofield, after throwing a crooked grin Durant's way, gestured for his friends to go on. Passing Blake, he muttered, "Make sure you keep goin', Durant. Go far and wide and forget all about her."

Blake's gaze hardened. *Her.* He knew Schofield could only be referring to Ellen Farner. His association with Ellen had been brief and meaningless. Once, weeks back, he'd accepted Farner's invitation to dinner. The girl had been shy, even embarrassed in his company. He couldn't remember her saying more than a few polite words to him. Yet he had

to admit that he was very much aware of her presence
in the days that followed, and often she'd walked to his
end of the train after the wagons stopped in the evening.
He'd presumed that his talk with her father at dinner had
interested her. Farner had asked about the West and Durant
had told him what he knew, which was a great deal. Farner
had seemed impressed. Perhaps Ellen had been, too.

His horse saddled, Blake put thoughts of the girl from
his mind. As far as he knew it was good country ahead with
plenty of fresh meat to be had and water in good supply.
The idea of having only Sundown for company didn't worry
him. Loneliness had been part of his life these past two
years. He had learned to live with it, to accept it, and even
at times to enjoy it. It helped a little to blot out the past he
wanted to forget ... the woman who'd loved him. If Louise
Yerby had lived, he wondered how different things would be
now—without men like Schofield, Blunt and Carney, without
the smooth-talking, well-groomed Mike Stanton, without the
troubles of others crowding in on him. Blake realized that the
loss of Louise had accentuated his own failings. He didn't
possess the warm and pleasant manner of men like Mike
Stanton, so he found it difficult to break down the reserve of
people towards him. It was always a chore to try to get along
with others. There was a definite barrier between him and
others.

He stepped into the saddle, gave Sundown a pat down
the shoulder, and the eager-stepping big black stallion
moved off. Since the trail west led straight up the track
through the loose circle of the wagons, Blake Durant
prepared himself for curious stares.

He had no doubt that word had quickly spread of his confrontation with Roland Farner and the Stanton hands. The fact that he was moving on would prove to everyone in the train that he had lost out. He didn't much care, he told himself, but there was a galling sensation in defeat of any kind. But, to keep the peace ...

"Mr. Durant."

The call came from one of the wagons. Blake reined up and saw her standing there in the fire's glow, her long hair gleaming, her eyes wide with questions. She was young and beautiful and desired by many men in the wagon train.

"Yes, Miss Farner?" he said.

She came towards him, walking lightly, looking shy yet determined. Her gaze was steady, and her eyes probed his when she drew up against the side of his horse.

"You're going on?" she asked quietly.

"I think it's best," he said.

"They ordered you out, forced you to go?"

Blake smiled. "I didn't belong here anyway. I'm better off on my own."

He thought he saw a lift of disappointment in her eyes. She clasped her hands and looked down at them.

The fire's glow heightened the beauty in her face, a beauty he had seen completely bewitch Rick Trice and most of the others. How many had a secret longing for her he didn't know, but he sensed that many of the men, even the older ones, had their private dreams of her when they were alone.

"Do you prefer to be on your own then, Mr. Durant, instead of with friends?"

Blake shrugged. "Friends are hard to come by, Miss Farner, and here in this place they're sure hard to recognize. Maybe you'll know what I mean when you're older."

"I'm old enough now," Ellen said, her chin lifting. "I'm nineteen."

"It's a good age for learning," Blake said and gave her a wave. He looked back a few hundred yards farther on and saw her still standing beside the fire, tall and slender. He rode on.

CHAPTER TWO
"You Been Told, Ain't You, Drifter?"

Blake Durant spent a rewarding two days in the hills.
Soon after leaving the wagon train he had come upon a long
green valley that wasn't rutted by wheels. The grass was tall
and water was plentiful. The information he had been given
about this valley before striking out from Lusc had proved to
be correct in every detail. He killed deer and rabbit and he
caught fat brown trout in deep pools in a fast-moving stream.
He didn't miss the wagon train at all, in fact he reveled in
being alone in such a beautiful place.

On the second evening since taking leave of Farner's
outfit Blake struck camp beside a small creek. The big
black stallion was grazing and Durant was stretched out
listening to the familiar night sounds when the drumming of
hoof beats alerted him to the approach of visitors. He was
immediately on his feet and heading for the cover of a circle
of rocks to the right of Sundown when loud laughter brought
him to a halt. In the gray light he saw Art Schofield leaning
against a tree, gun in hand. Five yards away stood Jute
Carney, holding his gun at the ready, amusement streaked
in his lean-featured face. Then Jimmy Blunt appeared riding
casually up the trail Blake himself had blazed earlier in the
day. Behind Blunt's mount were two horses Blake recognized
as belonging to Carney and Schofield.

"See him run, Jute?" Schofield said. "Damn me, I ain't
seen no jasper move as fast since you sent a barkeep
skitterin' back in Lusc."

Jute Carney chuckled and pushed himself off a boulder. He took two steps towards Blake Durant before Blunt halted his horse behind Blake. Blake Durant turned just enough to give him a sight of all three.

"What the hell is it now?" he rasped.

"It's a showdown, drifter, between us and you," Schofield said. "You've been snoopin' on us." Art Schofield pushed back his battered hat. He had plenty of width to match his height, and his chest was deep.

"Nobody's been snooping, Schofield," Blake told him. "What else is on your mind?"

"Ain't no more'n that, Durant," Blunt said, propping from the saddle and rubbing his big hands down his shirt front. "We seen you these past two days, comin' and goin' and all the time pryin', seein' what we was up to, like maybe you didn't want to lose track of us for some reason. Got to the stage where Mike Stanton said he was sick of the sight of you. Them farmers were gettin' unsettled, expectin' trouble, so Mike asked us to pay you a call, give you some advice and see you on your way—crawlin' if there weren't no other way you'd listen."

Blake eyed him without replying. He knew with certainty that these three had jumped at the chance to come after him. But why were they so keen on keeping their enmity for him going? From the beginning there had been friction between them.

"What's Stanton really after?" he asked. "And why is he so damned worried about me? I'm a threat to what?"

"No threat," Jimmy Blunt said, positioning himself so Blake couldn't shift away from him without getting closer to Carney and Schofield. Blake saw Blunt's fists bunch and he noted how the powerful muscles on his forearms bulged.

"Nope, no threat," Carney put in as Schofield went on grinning, although a glint of something approaching uncertainty came into his eyes when Blake didn't show worry. Carney, the least of them physically, looked the most threatening as he worked to Durant's left, watching him with eagle eyes, lips curled, all the menace of a killer in his scarred face.

The fight started with Carney's move. Blunt threw himself at Durant's back. The weight of him buckled Blake's knees. Then Carney, diving low, caught him about the thighs. Schofield, gun held in readiness, called out, "Make it good, make it real damn good. Have this interferin' drifter realize that he ain't in no way wanted in these parts or any other parts."

Blake rocked under Blunt's blow on the back of his neck. Sharp pain shot into his head. Then Carney pounded short but vicious blows into his ribs. Blake went with the pressure of the attack until he was able to grasp the little man's hair. He jerked Carney's head up just as a punch from Blunt smashed home on the side of his head. But it was Carney who Blake Durant wanted to stop first.

He lifted the man's face up. Seeing fear reach into the man's ugly features, he slammed his fist home and when Carney rocked back he maintained his grip on him. His second punch broke bone in Carney's cheek and his third cut open Carney's mouth. In panic Carney wrestled free and went staggering away, blood flowing from his mouth. Broken teeth spilled to the ground. His howling was like the wailing of a trapped animal.

Blake turned. Blunt's next blow tore past his head and he felt the air of it. Then he pounded three of his own punches into Blunt's big face. Blunt came to a halt, surprised and hurt. Blake kept punishing him, aware all the time that Schofield, after having pushed Carney out of his way, had circled and was trying to move in, but the thrashing arms of the shocked and reeling Blunt stopped him. Blake kept after Blunt until he was a bleeding, groaning, doubled-over hulk of submission. Then Schofield made his move, eyes ablaze with hate, the determination to kill twisting his features. His gun bucked in his hand and Blake felt the burn of the bullet across his forehead. He caught a momentary glimpse of Schofield, closer than he'd expected him to be, and he backhanded the tall man away. Schofield let out a bellow of rage and Blake lunged at him. His right hand clubbed down twice, and Schofield's gun fell. Blake heard Carney rushing in from behind and he wheeled, fists swinging. Carney twisted and went past him. Blake tripped him, stepped away and drew his gun. He hadn't wanted this to develop into gunplay, but he could see no other way for it.

Blunt was propped against the boulder, blood running from a gash on his right eye, his nose twisted and swollen.

Carney, trying to rise, watched blood from his ruined face splatter on his hands. Art Schofield, the least hurt, had hate in him that distorted his face into an ugly mask.

Blake Durant said, "The fun's over, gents. Don't make me go on with it."

Blunt wiped a shirtsleeve across his face and growled a curse. Carney rose and looked anxiously about him. His face was a mess. Only Art Schofield looked capable of continuing the fight, given the chance.

"We took you too damned easy, Durant," he said. Then he added, "This time."

Blake stepped to him, grabbed him by the shirt and hurled him back, causing Carney to jump clear. "There'd better not be another time," Blake said. "I don't know what the hell Stanton's after, but I don't reckon it has much to do with helping other people. What's his stake in this drive? What's at the end of it for him?"

"A new town, what else?" Schofield said. "One without your kind, drifter. Mike's got his mind set on making something real big out there. He sees himself as top man of his own empire. So it's natural that he don't want your trouble-makin' kind about, oglin' the women, standin' tall, always buckin' him. He had them farmers eatin' out of his hand until you come along with your talk about Rinald's outfit, about Howie not lettin' anybody settle. You was told once to clear out and there wouldn't have been no trouble. But you couldn't take that good advice, could you, mister?"

"Maybe I still can't, Schofield," Blake said. "As for trouble, it's all been of your own making. But that didn't worry me before, it doesn't now, and it won't in the future. So pick up your scum friends and get to hell out of here. Don't come back. If you do, so help me, Schofield, you'll learn that what happened here was an ants' picnic to what'll happen next time."

Schofield scowled. Jute Carney, his sleeve working overtime in an attempt to clean his face, suddenly dived at Blake Durant again. Blake gave a grunt of annoyance and met his charge with a swinging gun. The butt cracked down on the side of Carney's head and sent him sprawling again. Blunt made a quick move but Blake's gun rose to cover him.

Then all the anger which until that moment Blake Durant had been striving to control erupted within him. He grabbed Blunt and pitched him down the trail. Schofield shifted anxiously away, hands lifted in surrender.

Blake growled, "Get Carney out of here. Now! Move, damn you!"

Schofield reached down, picked up Carney effortlessly from the ground and tossed him roughly towards Blunt. Blunt caught at the unconscious hellion and slung him across his shoulder. Then, while Schofield pulled Blunt's horse free, Blunt growled:

"There'll be a next time, Durant. I found out you're good, real good, and I made a bad mistake in thinkin' otherwise. But next time, mister, so help me, next time—"

"Get!" Blake Durant snapped at him.

Blunt mouthed an oath and walked away, Schofield following. Blunt dropped Carney's body across the saddle, then they went on, with Blake watching them. When they were out of sight he saddled Sundown, broke camp and rode into higher country. He didn't think they'd be coming back, but to be on the safe side he struck camp in a cluster of rocks from where he could see far down into prairie country where, if Mike Stanton kept to his plans, the wagon train would appear the next day. Blake stretched out, studied his bruised fists and cursed. Then silence settled and he slowly let the tension ease out of him.

* * *

Mike Stanton, riding a beautiful white mare, came down from the hills looking content with himself. Perfectly groomed, he wore a wide-brimmed white hat which put his handsome face into shadow so he could take in the farmers settled about the fire without his check on them being noticed. He rode casually, his broadcloth coat flapping in the evening breeze, his trousers tucked into hand-tooled boots. Here was a man of substance and nobody seeing him could deny it. Confidence radiated from Stanton's face as he drew rein and slipped from the saddle. Then he made a show of dusting himself, smiling broadly at the men.

"Well now," he said to the farmers, "this sure is a sight to gladden a man's heart. You folk look so settled that I doubt that a storm or a fire or a stampede could disturb you. And that's exactly as it should be, for I've checked out the trail for twenty miles ahead and can tell you that everything is going according to plan. In fact, things are a lot better than I expected them to be."

"Then you discount Durant's talk about that bunch of marauders waiting ahead, Stanton?" Roland Farner put to him.

Stanton's gaze probed the darkness beyond the fire but he couldn't get a clear look at Farner's face. The man seemed to have an uncanny habit of getting some advantage on him.

"No," Stanton said, "I'm not fool enough to discount any rumor that comes my way, Farner. I've seen too many terrible things happen in my time to people who didn't listen when a warning was given. But I've seen no evidence to support what Durant said about marauders. You can't pay much attention to what his kind says."

"What kind is he?" Ellen Farner asked from her father's side. She was standing and the firelight washed over her, outlining the slenderness of her body. Stanton's sharp eyes appraised her for a moment. His voice remained genial when he answered.

"He's the kind who never comes to anything, Miss Farner. If you took a close look at his hands, you'd see that he hasn't spent much time earning his keep, although I did notice myself that the seat of his pants was uncommonly shiny."

Snickers of laughter came from the men.

"Do you judge a man on the state of his hands and trousers?" Ellen asked, a hint of sharpness in her voice.

Mike Stanton smiled at her and spread his hands over the fire. "I'd be a complete fool to do that, wouldn't I? Seeing that my own hands aren't calloused. But they're the hands of a man who takes responsibility on his shoulders, who doesn't spend his time in idle speculation but in planning things. I've ridden this trail before but I still take time to check it out. I leave nothing to chance. No person who follows me into untamed country can say I gambled with his life."

Stanton moved slowly around the circle, smiling at the farmers. As always, he knew he had them. It never took him long to win their confidence. He said, "And as for Durant's warning about Dan Rinald's outfit being ahead of us, well, I've made plans for that, too. You've probably noticed the absence of my hired hands from the camp tonight. Well, Schofield, Blunt and Carney, men who have my complete trust, are ahead scouting for the Rinald outfit. You can rest assured that in the event of trouble these men will prove themselves."

He walked on, again appraising Ellen.

"But who is this Dan Rinald? I've heard the stories about him the same as Durant did. And I've checked on him. Rinald, for all his notoriety, is nothing more than a cowardly criminal who preys on small outfits. He's afraid to show face in any town for fear of being arrested or shot down. Against him what have we got? You men, determined not to be pushed about, determined to get from life what you deserve and are willing to fight for. Can one band of cowardly scum worry men like you? I say no!"

There was a mumble of comment. Stanton went on smiling, looking confidently about him.

"I'm positive those outlaws don't worry a man in this wagon train. I checked you all out before I accepted your offer to lead this trek west. I wouldn't be here with you, willing to face risks with you, if I hadn't been of the opinion that you're men of the best caliber, men with courage, determination and vision. I told you about the trail I meant to take, and no one can deny that everything is just as I claimed it would be. In time you'll come to realize that everything I tell you is the truth—I don't act rashly, not when human life is at stake, and right now I'm telling you that we have nothing to fear on the score of Dan Rinald and his outlaws."

"What about the end of the trip, Mr. Stanton?" asked Roland Farner. "What about what Durant said about Colonel Howie?"

For the first time Stanton looked annoyed, but only briefly. He spread his hands in a gesture of resignation. "Durant, Durant, Durant! Does anything he say really amount to anything? What about this Colonel Howie? Does he own the whole country? Has he laid claim to every acre of ground outside of Washington? Would this country ever expand and grow into a nation if everybody stood back and let men like Howie take what they wanted? Would Kansas have grown? Would California have grown? Would any town west of the Platte River have grown? No. Emphatically not."

Mike Stanton removed his hat and ran a hand through his thick black hair.

He looked impressive standing there, shoulders wide and straight, his thin moustache adding strength to his fine, regular features. After a moment he shook his head.

"No, Colonel Howie has not laid legal claim to any land that I know of. He took some cattle into the untamed country and he let them stray. More through luck than good management he's built himself a sizeable cattle empire. He believes he's beyond reproach and doesn't have to answer to any person or government body. But he's wrong. When we reach the fertile valleys beyond this desert country you'll see land for the taking—and we'll take it, for it's our right. We're what you might call the chosen people, brought together so we'll have the strength to resist those who wish to wrong us. We'll build homes and schools and work the soil and in time we'll have a community others will be jealous of. So let's not have any more foolish talk about what Durant says, or what any other drifter says for that matter. And let's not worry about Colonel Howie or anybody else like him. We're doing no wrong and we don't have to answer to anybody. If Dan Rinald is stupid enough to attack us, then we'll show him quick that he's locked horns with the wrong crowd. But we must stick together and believe in each other, trust each other. Anything short of that will mean failure for all of us."

The farmers sat quietly, most of them looking to Roland Farner for direction. But the burly farmer merely sat hunched forward, arms folded, his brow rutted with thought. Ellen whispered something to him and Farner's head lifted. Stanton looked in the direction of Farner's gaze and saw his three men riding back to camp.

Stanton moved away from the crowd of farmers and walked up the wagon clearing. But when Schofield and then the bruised and gashed Carney and Jimmy Blunt came into the glow of light, Stanton's lips tightened and his eyes narrowed to slits. For a moment he seemed completely taken aback. Then, as he noticed Roland Farner rising and hurrying in his direction, he cursed and went on.

Before his men could come out of the saddle, Stanton growled, "What the hell happened?"

Schofield looked heavily at Carney and Blunt and said, "Durant jumped us. He must've seen us comin' and got the drop on Jimmy. Then, when Jute and me went in, he dodged away and tricked Jute. Damn him, Mike, he's sneaky."

Mike Stanton glared furiously at him. "You mean to tell me, damn you, that Durant—"

Stanton cut himself short as Roland Farner and two other farmers hurried up. Stanton looked fiercely at Schofield, then Farner, drawing to a halt, said, "I heard mention of Durant, Mr. Stanton. Is he causing more trouble?"

"Nothing we can't handle," Stanton grunted. "This is no business of yours."

"But by the look of your men, Stanton, they ran into some bad trouble. Surely, if Durant interfered with them while they were out checking the trail for Dan Rinald, it's the business of us all."

Schofield frowned at first, then looked relieved. "Yeah, Farner, Durant made a nuisance of himself when we were doin' just that. Mike said for us to check out Rinald just in case, and I guess we were just too busy at that and forgot about Durant. Then he jumped us and showed himself up as a real damned mean-livered hellion. If we meet up with him again, by hell, I'm going to kill him."

Ellen Farner had walked over and now she looked shocked at the damage done to the faces of Blunt and Carney. It was evident to her, despite her lack of contact with trouble of this sort, that Blake Durant had more than held his own against three men. Whether, as Schofield said, he got the jump on them or not, she felt relief over the fact that Durant had won out.

She asked, "And what happened to Mr. Durant, Mr. Schofield? Is he as badly hurt as your friends?"

Schofield's eyes blazed, then Blunt said, "Nope, ma'am, he ain't bad hurt. He tricked us and fought unfairly. We didn't have much chance, taken unawares as we were."

Ellen sent a probing look Mike Stanton's way. Composed again after his initial confusion, he said, "It looks like Durant really means to make trouble. But we can't let that get in the way of our plans. However, I must now bring to light the real reason why I wanted Durant to leave this train. He's a killer. Art remembered seeing him in Lusc when he shot down a man in cold blood. We didn't think it was any of our business out here so we just forced him to leave.

"I thought it better" Stanton went on "to disguise our real reason for wanting him to go, to save further worry in the train. But the fact remains that he's a murderer, and what he's done tonight just about confirms it. From now on, Blake Durant is banned from any contact with this outfit. I say he's to be shot on sight if he shows his face around here again."

Ellen looked horrified. "Then you don't intend to give him a chance to speak up for himself, Mr. Stanton?"

"Durant's had all the chances he deserves, and you can see what he made of them. Once and for all, Ellen, get it into your head that Durant is no good. He might have impressed you with his talk about the places he's been and the things he's done, but that was all talk. I know he spoke a great deal about himself when he had dinner one night with you and your father. But take it from me, Durant is the breed of man who gave the West its bad name in the first place. His kind take what they want. If anybody bucks them, as my men did a few days ago, he has to even the score. By hell, he'll pay for this."

Stanton waved for his trio of gun hands to move off.

When they were gone he turned to Ellen and her father. Two other farmers, Sel Watson and Tom Legarde, had withdrawn, more curious about the mauling Carney and Blunt had received than anything else.

Stanton said, "Ellen and Mr. Farner—you've got to remember that sometimes I have to be blunt. I've got a wagon train to get through and we'll have some hard experiences before the trip is over. So, although I apologize for my hard manner just now, please remember that this is not a milk-and-honey country. Not yet. It will be when we make it that way, but until then trust in me and don't go against me in anything. I'm sure you'll find out in the long run that you've done the right thing."

Stanton said goodnight and moved off to the side of his wagon. He stopped there and bit off the end of a thin cigar. Shoving the cigar between his mobile lips, he snapped out a curse. But only when he saw that Farner, Watson, Legarde and Ellen had moved off did he confront Schofield again, as the top hand was unsaddling his horse.

"What the blazes did happen, damn you? You were sent to teach Durant a lesson, to make sure he didn't come back. Instead of that you look as though you ran into a band of hostiles. Now you've shown Durant up in that girl's eyes as something big and brave. By hell—"

"Durant beat us fair," Jimmy Blunt said. "We had him cornered and were all set to take him apart. But he didn't run and he didn't beg. He proved himself about the best damn fighter I've ever come up against. We'd do better to admit that to ourselves in case there's more trouble with him later on. Taking him on anything near even terms is a mistake we shouldn't ever make again."

Art Schofield glared at Blunt but Carney's silence brought a deeper frown to Stanton's face. He turned to Blunt.

"Are you afraid of him, Jimmy?"

"No," Blunt said, and then he rubbed his swollen jaw. "I'm not scared of him. I'm only saying if I meet him again, I'm giving him no chance at all. I reckon we should all agree on that. Durant's good—big, fast and tough. A bullet is the only way to stop him."

Stanton eyed Carney. "That your opinion, too, Jute?"

Carney shrugged. "I wanted to cut him down first try. I don't see why you should give anybody a chance. If you don't want him in your hair, kill him."

Stanton nodded in agreement then he looked along the side of the wagon to make sure they were still alone. Confident that no one could overhear him, he lowered his voice and said:

"Well, we'll meet up with him again, make no mistake about that. Durant's heading our way and he knows this trail as well as I do. So he's got something on his mind which just might be linked up with Colonel Howie. If so, then the sooner Durant's dead and buried, the better all round."

Schofield looked relieved again. "Is it just the girl that's been worryin' you, Mike?" he asked.

Stanton scowled at him. "I'll take Ellen Farner any time I like and to hell with her or her father and the rest of them. No, I've been suspicious of Durant from the first moment he linked up with us, coming out of the distance and giving us no explanation but that he was heading west. In the very beginning I should have made him talk more. But no matter; the mistake was made and another was added to it tonight. They're the last two mistakes we'll make, by hell, or you'll answer to me personally."

Mike Stanton flipped his wide-brimmed white hat into the wagon and unbuckled his gunbelt. When he climbed up into the wagon leaving his three men standing there looking worried, his mind was on a great many things that had nothing to do with Ellen Farner and Blake Durant. He was thinking ahead, to the time all his dreams and ambitions would be fulfilled. In that frame of mind he went to sleep.

CHAPTER THREE
Mistaken Identity

For three more days Blake Durant kept an eye on the wagon train. They were in harsher country now, a section that had tested many adventurous travelers before. Fine white dust hung in a stifling cloud above the wagons and he knew from his own experiences that the nostrils of animals and men would be caked with the stuff. The sun was a ball of hell and the miles stretched on endlessly. Time didn't matter here; the country gave off a sense of timelessness. By the second day Blake knew that the men pushing on below would have forgotten all but the heat, the dust and their aching muscles. Their talk would be confined to mumbled complaints and an occasional prayer that the misery would soon end.

On the afternoon of the third day since his violent meeting with Blunt, Carney and Schofield, Blake broke into fertile country again. Suddenly, instead of dry blustery winds and oppressive heat, the morning was cool, with a light wind coming through tall timber on the banks of a narrow, slow-running stream. Blake let Sundown thread his way through the timber. What did Stanton have in the wind? he wondered. Did he really want to form a new settlement and consequently needed men like Watson, Farner and Legarde? Did he have the vision and ambition of other adventurers who'd struck into the heart of the wilderness to carve out a community for others to come and share?

Blake Durant doubted it.

There was something too deliberate and studied about Stanton's manner. He felt there was a hardness behind the man's veneer of respectability. And there was the fact that Stanton had brought along with him hard-core types like Schofield, Blunt and Carney. Yet wouldn't he himself, on an adventure like this, bring fighting men along, men who would take a chance and not shy away from the spilling of blood should it prove necessary to kill?

Blake swung off Sundown and let the horse drink. He filled his canteens and stacked them in his saddlebag, then he stood and breathed in deeply. This was his kind of country. A little ahead he saw the hills break into gorges and ravines. Up there waterfalls would add their soothing sound to the countryside.

He waited until Sundown had finished, then he led the stallion from the water. The wagon train with all its complex problems was not really his worry. From here on the trail would be easy riding for another hundred miles at least. Then there would be a second stretch of desert, a little tougher than this one. Then would come Colonel Howie's country.

Blake pushed his hat back and mopped sweat from his brow The heat of the last three days was still in him. He walked Sundown, giving the black stallion a well-earned rest, and headed for the heart of the hills. Up there would be meat. And shade. And cover. The last was important, for there was every chance that Dan Rinald would sight him and decide to make trouble.

The wagon train would be coming up fast behind him and would probably reach this same creek at the end of the day. If Rinald struck then, when the farmers were weary, he might have an easy victory.

Blake pushed the worrisome thoughts from his head. Time enough later for doing something about that. He struck north and made his camp in a wild peach grove where a rock spring provided clear, cold water. Within minutes he felt the tension leaving his body. Lying back, he closed his eyes against the sun glare overhead. No sooner had his lids shut than he felt the warmth of the sun lessening. A cloud across the sun? His instinct for trouble said no and he opened his eyes just in time to see the huge bulk of a man coming down on him.

Blake rolled. The big man's boots hit the ground with a heavy thud and a grunt came from him. Turning on his side and reaching for his gun, Blake saw a length of tree limb descending on his head. Too late he began to roll again and the branch struck him across the left shoulder.

Fierce pain lanced through his shoulders and neck. A second blow missed by inches as Blake kicked out desperately. His right boot knocked the branch from the big man's fist, and for a brief moment the giant stood there, his huge chest swelling, his neck muscles taut. Sweat and blood ran down his face and his eyes were glazed with madness. Blake reached for his gun but his holster was empty. His Colt lay ten feet away.

The giant lurched forward, not as quickly now as when he had begun his attack. Yet Blake hadn't struck back. Getting to his feet and circling, Blake heard the big man suck in his breath laboriously, as though his lungs were tortured for air. Then the lumbering giant closed on him, cornering him against a huge boulder. His huge fists rose and came down powerfully. Blake shifted and the giant pounded the rock face and let out a howl of pain.

Blake slammed two of his heaviest blows into the man's bloodied face and sent him staggering. The punches were heavy enough to knock out most men, but the giant was still on his feet.

Blake, using his superior speed, weaved out of the way of the big man's swinging arms and kept battering him with well-placed energy-sapping straight lefts and rights. For minutes the giant withstood this barrage of punishment and Blake could feel his fists bleeding when suddenly the giant went down on one knee. Blake hesitated, wanting to know the reason for the man's anger, but all he saw was a face torn with hate and desperation, a face sagging with weariness.

He said, "What the hell is this all about?"

The giant looked at him through his one open eye, then he threw himself forward in an attempt to get his hands around Blake's throat.

Blake stepped back and drove his knee into the side of the man's head. The giant fell, groaning, then he tried to lift himself, but he fell to his hands and knees, and lay still.

Blake walked to his Colt and picked it up. He'd come to grips with some big men in his life, but none could match the ferocity of this man. He'd won out, but he knew that if the giant had his normal strength he would have pounded Blake into the ground and left him mauled beyond recognition.

But why the attack?

Blake went across to him and with a great effort turned the man onto his back. He saw now that the huge body had been beaten badly, leaving bruises on every part of his chest, neck and arms. One wrist seemed to be broken and the other was badly swollen. His face was marred so badly there was no telling his age.

Blake looked up at the huge boulder from which the giant had jumped. Another second and he knew he would have been pounded unconscious by the big boots of the man. An involuntary shudder went through his body. He walked to Sundown. The horse was quiet after a bout of stomping and snorting. Blake pulled a rope from the saddlehorn and trussed the giant to a tree stump. Then he climbed past the boulder and followed the trail the giant had used. He was about to end his search, wanting to be where he could keep an eye on the big man, when he saw a woman propped up in shade against a pine trunk. Her clothes were in shreds. Blake figured that she was about thirty years of age; town-plump and badly hurt.

She wore heavy rouge which from a distance hid the bruises on her face but up closer was insufficient to hide the fact that her skin was torn and bruised. Blake pulled off his range coat, wrapped it about her shoulders and stood back.

The woman stirred. At first all she did was work her mouth and then fresh blood trickled between her white teeth. Her clothes, although torn badly, were expensive as far as Blake could make out. Her shoes were high-heeled and certainly ridiculous footwear for this type of country. Despite her condition, her eyes were curious.

"Who are you?" she asked and touched his range coat which fell from her shoulders to expose her high breasts. She pulled the coat up and smiled as if acknowledging his consideration of her.

"The name's Blake Durant. What about you, ma'am?"

"Ma'am?" she repeated and her smile widened. "It's been a long time since I've been afforded that kind of consideration, Mr. Durant." She extended her hand. "Would you help me to my feet? I'm not as badly hurt as my appearance might make you think."

Blake took her hand and she winced as he helped her up. She stood there, brushing her hair back, careful to keep the range coat over her nakedness. Then she looked about her, almost casually.

"There was a man with me," she said. "Have you seen him?"

"A big man? He tried to smash my head in."

"And failed, I see." She looked him over boldly and made no attempt to conceal her admiration.

"Yeah, he failed, but mostly because he was hurt and out on his feet. I have him roped down the trail. Friend of yours?"

"Companion," she answered with no feeling. Then she moved closer to him and sighed wearily. "Croft came from Lusc with me. He had nobody else to go with and I could see no problem in bringing him along."

She walked up and down as if working strength back into her long slim legs. If it had not been for the heavy rouge on her face, Blake thought, she would have looked beautiful. But the makeup gave her a rough, hard quality, and she showed more self-confidence than he expected to find in women. Her gaze met his squarely and behind her eyes he recognized a defiance that was disconcerting.

"We must set him free," she said. "Being roped like this would hurt him more than it would most people. He's very gentle and must be treated gently."

Remembering the pounding of Croft's fists on the boulder and the swish of the branch which might have killed him, Blake shook his head. "He stays tied, ma'am."

"The name is Lil. Lil Anderson. And we can't keep him tied. You'll have to trust in me. Croft will do no harm to anyone who doesn't harm me. We had some trouble and he was beaten mercilessly. I don't know how he survived at all, but he beat off five men and then he carried me to safety. I passed out while he was still running with me and they were trying to kill us. But it seems he escaped them."

"What five men?" he asked.

"Dan Rinald and his scum friends, Mr. Durant. If you've been in these parts any length of time then you've heard of them. Rinald is an outlaw and a killer; a mean, vicious man."

Lil shuddered and then, her lips tight, she walked down the trail and went on talking as they made their way back to Croft. "It all started in Lusc, Mr. Durant. Croft and his friend, Lonnie Rolls, a miserable little runt of a man, came into town and Rolls robbed the saloon. He was seen doing it and a crowd attacked him. Croft, who did everything Rolls asked of him through a distorted sense of loyalty, went to Rolls' aid. A gun butt ended the fight, but not before Rolls had grabbed a gun and shot down a deputy. Rolls was hanged, but I felt sorry for this big, mentally disturbed giant, so I hid him. It wasn't long before he was discovered and we had to make a run for it. I had mules already packed and we made good our escape. On the way I discovered that Croft had the mind of a child and was gentle and innocent. He had trailed all over with Rolls, doing whatever was asked of him. When I told him Rolls was dead and I needed him he tacked onto me. He substituted me for Lonnie Rolls as easily as you might exchange a tired horse for a fresh one, Mr. Durant."

She smiled again but it was a weary effort and brought out
more strongly the lines under her eyes and along her mouth.

"Then Dan Rinald found us and wasted no time showing
that he wanted me. I tried at first to get him to wait, telling
him lies about myself and making promises for the future.
But Dan Rinald is an impatient man and he soon saw
through my scheme. He dragged me off but Croft heard my
screams and there was one big fight before Croft beat Rinald
and his four men into the ground, but not before he was
brutally bashed himself. Somehow he got me away. Then I
passed out."

Her smile did nothing to relieve the tension which had
taken hold of Blake the moment he came into contact with
Croft. Despite her assurance that Croft was a gentle giant,
he had no plans for untying him.

They circled back along the trail Croft had bloodied and
came into the shady grove to find the big giant propped
against the tree stump, the rope tight about his massive
chest. His hot gaze swung to Durant and there was no doubt
in Blake's mind that, if free, this giant would rush him and
continue their fight.

Lil walked to Croft and pushed the strands of lank hair
back from his forehead. She knelt beside him and stroked his
hair for a time before she asked Blake for water. When Blake
put a canteen into her hand, she said:

"We escaped from Rinald and his hellions late yesterday so you can understand, Mr. Durant, just what kind of hell Croft has been through, beaten up as he was to the point of exhaustion, then having me to worry about. I suppose he thought you were one of Rinald's men. You'll have to forgive him."

Blake said nothing. Croft's fierce look remained fixed on him and his chest heaved against the rope.

Lil fed him water and wiped the blood from his face. Blake couldn't help wincing when he saw the mass of welts and bruises on the giant's face.

Lil said, "Croft, I want you to listen to me. Mr. Durant is our friend. He's not one of those bad men. Mr. Durant found me and helped me as best he could. Now he's going to help you. We'll get out of this wilderness and we'll all be friends and stay together."

Blake was of no mind to fall in with this scheme but for the moment he let Lil Anderson have her way. Slowly the hate died in Croft's eyes.

"You understand now, Croft, don't you? You're not to fight with Mr. Durant. He's our friend, just as Lonnie Rolls was your friend and I'm your friend." Lil turned to Blake. "Have we anything to eat?"

Blake fetched jerky and unleavened bread from his saddlebag and handed it to her.

But Lil stood and said quietly, "Please, Mr. Durant, you give it to him. It's the quickest and best way to win his confidence. Then untie him."

Blake looked heavily at her. "I'll decide on doing that in my own time, Miss Anderson."

"Suit yourself. I'm only trying to help, Mr. Durant. You have a gun which I presume you know how to use, and Croft is still far from strong. Surely, with that much advantage you can't be frightened of him."

Her eyes gleamed with challenge. Blake swore under his breath and tossed the jerky down to Croft. He looked at it and then at Lil and only when she nodded did he lower his head and pick up the jerky from his roped hands with his teeth. Drawing his head back he munched heartily and his eyes went soft with obligation to her, but not to Durant.

Durant watched him. When the big giant gave him a crooked smile, he took out his knife and cut the rope. Croft immediately tore the bonds free and looking straight at Durant, smiled broadly. Then he coiled up the rope and handed it up to Blake. Durant took it from him and stepped back, still uncertain, still not ready to trust the man. Croft rose to his feet, worked his massive shoulders a moment and breathed in deeply. Then he walked across to Sundown and began to stroke the black stallion's head. Sundown pulled away at first but soon submitted, and Lil, turning to Durant with a satisfied smile on her bruised face, said:

"Perhaps we can now begin to make plans, Mr. Durant. You haven't told me yet what you're doing out here, where you're heading or why. I'm very curious to learn all about that ... and about you."

Blake, still keeping an eye on Croft, said, "I'm making my own way west for reasons which are nobody's business but my own. But I think I can help you and Croft before I push on."

Lil frowned at him. "We're heading west, too, in search of a new life. I've been told there are good towns past the big desert. It's there that I aim to put my past behind me. So, unless you have something definite ahead of you, why don't you throw in your lot with us? I'm sure that once Croft gets to know you, you'll find him a big asset, especially in inhospitable communities."

"I'm not looking for inhospitable communities, Miss Anderson," Blake told her. "In fact, I'm not looking for any communities at all in the way you mean it. Anyhow, I doubt that your information will bear up with the facts. Past the big desert there's nothing but a cattle ranch run by one man, a man who doesn't take kindly to people crowding his range. So if all you have in front of you is the hope of a new life, I suggest that you turn back."

"You mean walk back to Lusc, Mr. Durant?"

Blake bit his lip. "How the hell did you get this far?"

"On my mules, as I told you before. But Dan Rinald took the mules and made off with all my personal possessions and our food. So we're stranded out here and must rely on you." She smiled, a brittle, over-confident smile that annoyed Blake.

He said, "There's another way, Miss Anderson."

She frowned and clutched the range coat tighter around her lush body. "What other way? Have you the power to manufacture a buckboard, a team of horses, provisions, water?"

"There's a wagon train coming up," Blake said. "A dozen wagons packed with farming people heading west. I'll take you to them in the morning and you can work things out for yourselves from there."

Lil's gaze hardened and her mouth thinned. Blake realized then what kind of a woman she was. The exposure of her past was written in her features.

Lil had left an "inhospitable" town. But Blake liked Lusc. The people were reserved with strangers but not openly bitter. If a person stood his ground and pulled his weight, he would find a helping hand there.

"I want no part of wagon trains or farmers," she said. "I've had my fill of that kind of people. I couldn't expose myself to the vicious, hating eyes of suspicious farming women and to their gossip. Nor to the sickening looks and vile thoughts of their stupid men. No, I'm afraid you found us, Mr. Durant, and you're stuck with us."
40

Lil moved about, ignoring Croft, although Blake was aware that the big, moon-faced giant didn't for a moment take his eyes off her.

"Mr. Durant," Lil continued as she reached the other side of the clearing, "I've just been through a terrible experience but I'm sure you'll admit that I've borne up well under the strain." She smiled again, becoming more sure of herself. "That's simply because I've always been subjected to terrible experiences at the hands of men. But I know them for what they are. I want no part of them. So I'm going on, on foot, if you force that on Croft and me. We'll make out, I assure you, and we'll avenge ourselves on Rinald when next we meet up with him. So, Mr. Durant, we'll share your camp for the evening and we'll let you go on your way in the morning. All right?"

Blake had no answer, but he knew he couldn't ride away and leave a half-crippled giant and a destitute woman to fend for themselves in wild country. Rather than let her keep badgering him, he crossed to Sundown, pulled him free of the shade and then, swinging into the saddle, he said, "Wait here."

"Where are you going?" Lil asked.

"To get some fresh meat. Make a fire. Use dead wood that won't let off too much smoke. I should be back in about an hour."

With that Blake rode up the trail and out of sight.

As Croft turned and frowned after him, Lil crossed to him and told him to sit down. She then made him take off his tattered shirt and she examined his wounds. Later, with all the blood washed from Croft's massive body, Lil sighed wearily. It was clear to her that Croft, despite his strength, wouldn't be able to move very far on foot for several days. She looked down into the empty prairie country. Tomorrow, if Durant spoke the truth, a wagon train would come through. A wagon train from Lusc.

She wondered if any of the men in the train had visited the Lusc saloon and seen her there. Or if any of their women had discussed her at their campfires, wrinkling their noses in disgust for what she was and what she did. Lil smiled bleakly. It was a hard life, but it could get no worse. She had Croft, and now there was Blake Durant.

She told herself that if she didn't have Blake Durant completely in her power by morning it wouldn't be for lack of trying. Moving away from Croft, she told him to lie still and rest, then she collected wood for the fire.

* * *

Mike Stanton drew rein at Roland Farner's wagon and called for the farmer to come out. It was dusk of their last day in the desert. Mike Stanton had hoped to be out in the fertile country before this but wheel trouble on two of the wagons had caused several hours of lost time.

Farner poked his head out of the canvas and studied
the wagon boss blandly. For the last few days, Farner
had watched Stanton closely and his confidence in the
man's leadership had suffered as a consequence. It was
nothing that Farner could put his finger on, but during the
hazardous desert crossing, Stanton had not been much of
an encouragement to the struggling wagon drivers. He had
in fact been away on several occasions when decisions
about the trail had to be made. It was Farner himself who
had taken command and was responsible for the wagon train
getting this far without serious delay.

Mike Stanton removed his hat and flattened his moist hair
onto his head. His gaze settled on Farner and amusement
gleamed in his eyes.

"Turned in already, Roland?" he asked. "So early?"

"It's been one hell of a day," Farner said. "We had wheel
trouble with Watson's wagon again and an axle broke
on another. I looked for you, hoping to come to some
arrangement about slowing the pace. The oxen are bearing
up as well as can be expected, but some of the younger
children and older women are all in. Another day in this heat
and I'm afraid some of them may die."

Stanton nodded gravely and studied the clear sky. There
wasn't a cloud to be seen and the air was so hot he had to
loosen the collar of his shirt. Yet he looked no more weary
than when Farner saw him set out that morning.

"Tell them the worst of their hardship is behind them," Stanton said. "I've checked the trail ahead and it bears out what my map says. By noon tomorrow, after an early start in the morning, we'll make camp at the river. From there on it's good going, possibly the best any of you people have seen. Green valleys, cool winds, plenty of water and feed, and so beautiful it will take your breath away."

On hearing this Farner brightened. He turned and then called across his shoulder, "Ellen, come out please. I have wonderful news."

Ellen appeared a moment later, holding a brush with which she'd been working the day's dust out of her hair. Now her hair hung long and gleaming to her shoulders. Mike Stanton eyed her with undisguised admiration and said:

"Roland, what I just said about the country ahead is true, but when talking about beautiful things, how could I go past making a mention of your daughter? Ellen, you're radiant tonight. I honestly don't know how you do it. When everybody else is jaded, nerves on end, you manage to look as cool as creek water under the shade of elms."

Ellen blushed despite herself. For many days now she had been aware of Mike Stanton's interest in her. Earlier on the trip, the young men in the wagon train had paid her many compliments. She didn't take any of them too seriously, but she enjoyed receiving them. Then, three days ago, after Blake Durant had gone on his way, the young men began to keep their distance.

At first she had taken little notice of it, putting it down to tiredness on their part or worry about the future. But last night, thinking about it all again, she wondered if something else had happened, such as Mike Stanton letting it be known that he didn't want anyone to show interest in Ellen.

"Thank you, Mr. Stanton," she replied.

"Mike is the name, Ellen. None of us has to stand on ceremony out here. I've just been telling your father that water is ahead, enough to drown ourselves in. After the last few days I think we all deserve a good spell. It'll help our nerves settle down again, and it'll lift our spirits to where they should be. By noon tomorrow, we'll be in the land of milk and honey, just as I promised you. And, Ellen, I want to be the first to show that country to you. Will you do me the honor of riding ahead when we sight the creek? I want to be the first to kill a deer or maybe an elk, and I'd like you to share my moment of triumph."

Ellen frowned and glanced at her father. Roland Farner had a faraway look in his eyes and she knew he was caught up in dreams of his future.

"But there will be so much to do, Mr. Stanton. Everybody will be needed to—"

"Nonsense. You've done more than your share now, riding with the men, relieving your father with the wagon, cooking and looking after the smaller children. I've watched you carefully, Ellen."

Stanton continued "You're a woman who'll do your father proud. You were born to come out into this country because in time you'll be the first lady of it. I'll call for you when I get word from the scouts that the creek is in sight."

Mike Stanton tipped his hat to her, turned his white mare and rode away before she could refuse him. Turning to her father, Ellen saw that he was still dreaming. With a shrug she went back into the wagon. But she put her comb down now and inspected her face in the small hand mirror her father had bought for her in Lusc. She decided she was beautiful, there was no use denying it out of a sense of humility. Yet the praise and attention of Mike Stanton somehow annoyed her. His manner suggested that he only had to decide he wanted her and she'd be his. Well, she told herself, Mike Stanton was in for a great shock. Ellen Farner was a woman who made her own decisions. She put down the mirror and turned around as her father poked his head in. He said:

"I'm going to tell everyone, Ellen. We'll organize a party for tomorrow night. We'll have music and dancing. And it won't hurt to turn out a jar of something stronger than coffee, eh?"

His face was so filled with happiness, like a boy's, that Ellen couldn't bring herself to dampen his spirits. She said, "A party will be nice, Pa. Everybody needs it."

"So get out that pretty dress you bought in town and show them what the Farners are bringing to the wilderness. By Hannah, things are on the turn and I guess we've got to thank Mike Stanton for most of it. Everything he said has turned out right. I feel disgusted with myself for the doubts I had."

Roland Farner hurried on his way and Ellen climbed over the wagon seat and leaned against the canvas. The wind was hot and the night quiet. She looked towards the hills in the distance and with a shock realized that she was wondering what Blake Durant was doing.

CHAPTER FOUR
End of a Peace Trail

Blake Durant and Croft stood gazing west into the dark hills. Croft, looking completely recovered from his ordeal, carried a frown that he turned onto Durant. Blake, still not certain of the giant's loyalty, nodded.

"Yeah, I heard."

"Not far," mumbled Croft and he looked about for a moment before stooping to pick up a solid deadfall log. He weighed the log in his two huge hands before he turned to take a position close to Lil Anderson. Lil, who had just finished cleaning up after their breakfast, recognized the worry in Croft's face and asked:

"What is it? Is something wrong?"

The big man gave no answer but his brow was rutted deeply. Blake Durant drew his gun and checked it.

"What is it, Mr. Durant?" Lil got to her feet and pushed past Croft.

Before Durant could answer, Croft placed a firm but gentle hand on Lil's shoulder and shook his head. "Stay back," he muttered.

Lil obeyed without question because the expression in Croft's face alarmed her.

Lil again looked at Durant who was leading Sundown across the clearing. When Blake tethered the horse behind a cluster of rocks, she called out, "For hell's sake, what is it?"

"Croft and I heard noises above us on the slope. But I've seen no movement, although I don't think either of us was mistaken. It could have been some foraging animal."

"No." Croft shook his head and the vacant look was gone from his eyes.

Lil looked fearfully at Croft and went on, "He might not know everything that goes on about him, Mr. Durant, but he has an uncanny foresight about trouble. Last time Rinald attacked us, we would have been completely overpowered if Croft had not—"

"Be quiet, Lil," Blake Durant said suddenly. He left Sundown and hurried across the clearing. But he hadn't reached cover on the other side of the rocks when a rifle blasted.

Lil let out a cry but Croft pulled at her shoulder and worked her against the side of the biggest boulder. Then, without a word, he walked ahead, his huge body shielding her.

Seeing the giant stride towards the track leading up the slope, Blake Durant cut him off.

"Wait here, Croft."

Croft's steel-eyed look played over Blake's face for a moment, then he shouldered him aside and went on. Croft was twenty feet up the trail when the other guns spoke. Bullets ripped down. Blake broke into a run, working slightly off the track and breaking through the brush. Croft stopped momentarily and Blake saw his face jolt under a rise of pain. He also saw a patch of blood appear on the man's tattered shirt. Then a bullet grazed his own forearm. Cursing, Durant went farther into the brush, looking for a target.

When he reached the extreme end of the slope, Blake stopped. The shooting had stopped. There had to be a deep hollow where the attackers had left their horses. Hoping to get to them and set them running, he dragged himself up a rock and flattened on its top. The sun shone directly into his eyes causing him to blink. But then, eyes shaded by the brim of his hat, he peered about, tensed and ready to fight.

Croft was still walking on, the patch of blood on his shirt becoming larger with every moment. But he walked straight and showed no pain. Blake watched him admiringly until he sighted movement directly in front of Croft.

A moment later a man's head appeared, then another. A third man broke cover to the right and then a fourth appeared above the first two. Blake swore when he saw that the four men were holding their fire, letting Croft walk into their trap.

Blake jumped down from the boulder and, throwing discretion to the wind, plowed through the thick brush towards Croft.

The big man heard him coming and stopped, staring sourly. But then he recognized Blake Durant and his face relaxed. He moved forward again and Blake had no recourse but to step into the open. As he ran, this time through less cluttered country, he called loudly, "Get down, Croft. Down!"

If Croft heard him, he paid Blake no heed. He stepped out of the knee-high brush and started across a short open space, a massive figure making as easy a target as any killer could want.

The guns opened fire again, and to Blake's surprise Croft went into a run, veering to the right where Blake had seen the third of the men crouched in readiness. Croft stopped momentarily. Blake could see a streak of blood on his scalp. Then the giant walked on, apparently not affected by his two wounds. Blake watched spurts of flame and puffs of smoke. Taking a deep breath, he plunged into the open again and fired, aiming at the positions the smoke had come from. He heard a man cry out in pain, then rise and stagger a few unsteady steps before he pitched down the slope on his chest. Blake went on, emptying his gun at the line of rocks before he dived for cover and refilled his Colt.

While he lay flat on his stomach, bullets whined over his head. He couldn't see Croft now but he could hear brush being trampled not far above him. His gun ready again, Blake jumped to his feet. He saw two men converging on Croft and the giant seemed ignorant of their presence. The big man suddenly halted. Lifting the stout stick above his head, he brought it down hard on the top of a boulder.

He then moved forward again, swinging the stick a second time. Now Blake could see the object of his fury, for a runt of a man broke cover and, shielding his head with a raised arm, fired off a shot at Croft. The giant took no notice of this and brought the stick down a third time. Blake heard an unearthly scream come from the runt before Croft grabbed him. With one hand he hurled him down the slope. The man smashed into the side of a boulder and rolled away, his head crushed. He didn't move.

The two above were apparently stunned into inaction by the brute power of Croft. Before they could react, Blake sprinted past Croft and, firing from the hip, sent them running. But another two men showed up on Blake's left and he wheeled, caught in their crossfire, to punch off fast shots. One of the slugs hit home and a hellion dropped to his knees, fired a bullet at the sky and fell forward on his face. When he didn't move the other turned and fled.

Blake switched his attention back to the other two, but they had gone on over the rim of the slope. By the time Blake got to the top of the rise, the sound of galloping horses came to him from the valley.

Blake halted. He had a throbbing pain in his forearm and gave a moment's attention to the wound to find it no more than a two-inch long gash that was bleeding freely. Blake took his bandanna from his neck and wrapped it around the wound. Unable to see any horses in the grove which began the long, grassy valley, he turned back on his tracks and sought out Croft.

Although he looked for several minutes he couldn't find the big man. He did, however, find the two men he had killed and the runt Croft had hurled to his death. Blake piled them together in the shade of some trees and continued his search. It was five minutes later before Lil appeared, her face white, her hands shaking.

Blake said, "It's all right now."

But this did nothing to compose Lil. She looked fearfully at the bloodied trio. Backing off, she kept shaking her head, her usual confidence in herself completely shattered. Blake told her to stay in the shade while he continued his search for Croft. Finally he found a bloodied section of brush that was heavily trampled. At the end of it, where rocks had been disturbed and a tree stump partly torn from the ground, he saw Croft's body. The giant's face was buried in the rubble and his hands were beneath him. Blake pulled Croft onto his back and sucked in his breath when he saw the gaping wound in Croft's chest. The giant was still breathing but his face had lost its color. Lil, who had been watching fearfully from the shade of the boulders, now came slowly forward, her face as white as Croft's.

"Is he ... is he dead?"

"Nope, but I'm damned if I know why not. Fetch some water while I try to get him into shade."

Lil moved away and Blake struggled across the clearing with the giant, dragging him by the shoulders, his heels cutting ruts in the ground. He propped Croft against a boulder, and while Lil washed the giant's head Blake tore his shirt free. Lil gasped when she saw the wound but Blake took no notice of her alarm and tended Croft as best he could. When he had the big man's chest bandaged, he stood away and looked down into the prairie country.

"They have a doctor with the wagons," he said.

Lil looked searchingly at him. "I won't go for help, not to the wagon train," she told him. "If they came from Lusc as you said, then some of the people are sure to have heard about me. I was thrown out of that town, branded an undesirable."

Blake held her look evenly and said, "If Croft doesn't get better care than we can give him here, he'll die, no matter how damn stubborn he is about it. I think you owe it to him to give him every chance."

Lil bit at her bottom lip. Tears came into her eyes when she saw Croft try to rise and then slump back again.

"I saw it all," she said. "He wouldn't let them come at me. He shielded me with his body and he must have known he had no chance."

"I think he knows more than we give him credit for. He took two bullets getting at one of them, a little runt who had the drop on him."

"That's Miers," Lil informed him. "A little cowardly scum."

"I don't give a damn who he was. You knew the others?"

"It was Dan Rinald who almost got you," Lil said. "He was the one on the right, high. The two who ran off with him were Parry Miller and Joe Elder."

"You found out a lot about them in one attack, Lil," Blake said tightly.

Lil smiled sadly. "Well, not actually in that one attack, Mr. Durant. Rinald was in Lusc at the same time I was. He tried to molest me behind the saloon one night. That was before Croft linked up with me. The others I knew only by name until they attacked me out here. And that's about all I want to know about them from now on."

Blake wiped sweat from his brow. Yet the cool wind from the slope made it pleasant enough here, bearable anyway.

"We'll have to wait," he said quietly. "I'd like to ride off and check out Rinald's movements. If he comes again, by hell, I want to be ready for him."

Lil knelt at Croft's side and dabbed his brow with a wet cloth. The big man opened his eyes, smiled at her and then looked directly at Blake Durant. Blake saw in that look none of the vacancy of the subnormal. Instead he saw a flicker of warmth.

Blake fetched Sundown and rode up to the rim of the slope. From there he could see down into the big valley. The timber was thick at the other end and a rise of dust still clung to the low branches of pines. Filling his gun, Blake Durant followed the trail of three horses. At the other end of the valley he saw where they had circled and gone south, where there were high hills and plenty of boulder cover. Rinald and his cronies had probably decided enough was enough. For the moment.

Retracing his tracks, Blake found Lil propped against a tree, her skirt tidily across her lap, his range coat covering only her shoulders and part of her bare breasts. Lil did not bother to cover her nakedness even when she saw him standing there. A gleam of interest came into her eyes.

"What have you decided?" he asked.

Lil shrugged. "Do I have a choice?"

"It's stay here and wait for the wagon train or let Croft die."

Lil bit her lip again and her look hardened. "You won't help anymore?" she asked.

"I've got my own plans made," he told her.

Lil pushed herself to her feet and looked scornfully at him. "Do you think as they do, that you're above me, Durant? Is that it?"

"I'm not given to making opinions on people I don't know, Lil. You've had it rough. Don't make it any rougher on yourself."

Lil sniggered at him. "Rough," she repeated and then she nodded as she turned away. "Yes, rough, but perhaps it was partly of my own making. I came out here because Croft was in trouble and at the same time he could help me get a new start. His loyalty to me would have given me the chance to make my way honestly. We could have got a little place and his strength and my shrewdness would have seen us through. But what is there now? He'll die and I'll be with people who know my past and hold it against me." She paused. "I wish you were a different kind of man, Blake Durant, one who isn't made of damned stone!"

Her smile had very little warmth in it. Blake decided she had finished her speech and he was pleased to let it stay at that. He struggled with Croft and finally got him across Sundown's saddle. Then, with Lil walking at his side, Blake led the black stallion. His only worry now was what kind of reception he would get from Mike Stanton and his men. If there was further violence he doubted if he would draw off.

He had suffered enough crowding and wanted only to be left alone. Blanking his mind to the pressures mounting up, he made for the creek.

* * *

The wagon train came out of the desert at high noon. Even from the shade of the trees a quarter mile from the leading wagon, Blake could see relief flood into the faces of the wagon driver and his wife. Blake recognized them as Sel and Bess Watson, solid people not apt to trust a person quickly, a pair who waited and let things come to them.

He called Lil to wake her up. When she stirred, he said, "Here come your friends."

Lil snorted at him and walked across to Croft. The big man was unconscious again, but his breathing was almost normal. Lil tidied her hair and drew in a deep sigh. "Then this is the end of the trail for us, Blake? You still intend to ride on alone?"

Blake nodded. "I had my trouble with this outfit, too. When they come up, let me do the talking. And don't argue if they try to ride me down. I'll handle them in my own way."

Lil frowned. "What kind of trouble, Blake? If they aren't friendly towards you, surely we can figure out something else. We can buy provisions from them, perhaps get two more horses. Croft will make it if we travel back slowly."

Blake shook his head. "I've got to go on," he said. He pushed Sundown from the shade and rode to a small rise in the direct path of the wagon. Now he could see the other wagons spread out, with oxen and steers packed together, some of the men walking, most of the women driving or in the back of the wagons.

He sighted the red hair of Ellen Farner gleaming against the backdrop of dust. Her father was at her side, burly and thoughtful, his curious eyes fixed on Durant.

Blake edged his horse over the rise and came out of the saddle. His movements masked by Sundown, he checked his gun and reholstered it. Then Roland Farner gestured for Ellen to draw rein and Ellen wheeled the covered wagon near to Blake.

Farner said, "Well, Durant, we didn't expect to see you again. If you're here to make more trouble, forget about it. Our tempers are frayed enough after what we've been through."

Blake looked beyond him to the other wagons drawing up. He saw Sel Watson bring his rifle from under the driving seat. To his right, Bob Coles motioned for his wife and daughter to retreat behind his wagon. Rick Trice, after checking out the widow Morrison's wagon, spurred his horse and reined up beside Farner's wagon. His young face was old with defiance.

Where's Stanton?" Blake asked.

"Gone ahead. We expected to meet him here." Farner looked frowningly about him, the absence of Stanton clearly worrying him.

"I've seen no sign of him," Blake said. "Which is all to the good. I've a favor to ask of you, Farner."

"Favor?" the farmer asked tightly.

Blake nodded and waved to Lil. As soon as she appeared from below the rise, Rick Trice gasped. "Why it's that Anderson woman, Mr. Farner. You know, the one they ordered out of Lusc."

"I see that, Rick," Farner said shortly and waited for Lil to draw level with Blake, who was immediately aware of the rustle of interest in the other wagons. He saw women looking sternly at each other, while the men did their best to conceal their interest in Lil.

"What's the favor, Durant?" Farner asked.

"I came upon them in the hills to our right. They'd been badly mauled by Dan Rinald and his outfit."

"They?" Farner asked, looking past Lil to the creek his straining oxen were impatient to reach.

"There's a man back there near dead. I'll make my report short and leave the rest for Miss Anderson to tell as she wishes later. Rinald left them without provisions or horses. Croft defended Miss Anderson as best he could before he was nearly battered to death. Then, early this morning, we were attacked by Rinald, probably in reprisal for what Croft handed out to his outfit. I killed two of those scum, Croft accounted for another. The other three made off. But I'm sure they didn't go far; in fact, I think their main interest is getting what they can from this wagon train."

Farner drew himself tall in the driving seat. His face was dark with thought and his hands were locked on the seat rail, his knuckles white under the strain of his grip.

"Why doesn't Croft come out and speak for himself?" Farner asked gruffly. "What is he afraid of here?"

"If he could walk, he'd be here," Blake said. "You'd best see for yourself."

Blake motioned for Lil to return to the creek. While the farmers craned their necks to get a better look at her, Blake shielded her as she walked. Croft was lying on his side now, still unconscious. At sight of him, Farner came down from the seat. Telling Ellen to stay back, he walked down the stony creek bed to the big man. He stood at his side for awhile and then he turned at the sound of movement. Rick Trice drew up. Giving Blake a guarded look, he drew Farner to the side. Blake couldn't hear what he whispered but immediately afterwards he heard Farner say gruffly:

"I know that, Rick. I saw him in Lusc, too. Who could miss him?"

"But he was with that Rolls jasper they hanged, Mr. Farner. Hell, if he rode with him, ain't he the same as him? And ain't the woman been trouble all along? You ain't gonna let her be where your daughter is, are you?"

"I'll decide on that for myself, Rick," Farner said shortly. "There appears to be a good deal more to learn here before any of us begins to make decisions."

Farner turned and confronted Lil. "You were attacked, Miss Anderson, by Dan Rinald?"

"Yes," she said.

"How did you know it was Dan Rinald?"

Lil smiled tightly. "Mr. Farner, I've known Dan Rinald for many years. Often, even under the eyes of the law, he's tried to win my regard. When I refused to have anything to do with him, he became mean. And when Dan Rinald gets mean, somebody suffers."

"Then perhaps his reason for being out here is only to take you off with him?"

Lil shrugged. Her eyes were steady when she said, "Dan Rinald is a thief before he's anything else, Mr. Farner. If I'm important to him it's only as a second consideration. He'll attack you, just as Mr. Durant says."

Farner accepted this without argument. "And Croft?"

"He's with me. He is a simple man, scarcely able to understand what goes on. He rode with Rolls but he couldn't possibly have known about the deviltry Rolls was always getting up to. In his way, I suppose Rolls needed Croft. But when Rolls died, thanks to my getting Croft away from a murdering mob of fools, he transferred his loyalty, love if you like, to me. I can't desert him now, not after all he's suffered on my behalf."

Rick Trice frowned at Lil. It was plain to Blake Durant that Trice was one of those young men who hadn't yet learned enough from life to feel tolerance.

"I think that as leader of the farmers you must make the decision, Mr. Farner," Lil said quietly. "My friend is so badly wounded that he may not regain consciousness. Mr. Durant has done all he can for us. So we're here, begging for your assistance." Lil looked severely at Trice. "I can only assure you of one thing. We don't want anything from you that we won't repay you for in time. A little food, and a ride. No more. In return for that Croft, when he gets on his feet, will do more work on your new settlement than six of you could do in the same time. As for myself, I'll do any chores you ask of me. One way or another we're going west, no matter what happens. You can take us with you or you can leave us here."

Farner frowned at her. "You know we can't do that, Miss Anderson."

"And we can't let you join up with us," said Sel Watson, appearing behind Farner. "My wife has already expressed her disgust with this woman. Bess is a good woman, a God-fearing woman. I will not subject Bess to the sight of this ... this woman!"

Lil straightened and glared past the red-haired farmer at the woman holding the horses steady. Bess tilted her head back and a stern look came into her eyes. Farner mumbled under his breath and the other farmers began to close in.

Then four riders suddenly came tearing up from the creek. At their head was Mike Stanton. As soon as he saw Blake Durant, Stanton unholstered his gun. Drawing rein, he worked his horse in behind Blake.

"Seems you don't listen to what you're told, Durant," he barked. "By hell, mister, you've asked for it now."

"Hold it," Farner called angrily and moved quickly to stand between Stanton and Durant. But by then a leering Jute Carney had drawn his gun and had it leveled on Blake, his mean little eyes filled with hate. Art Schofield, seeing Jute in control, swung down from his horse. Pushing Blake against Farner's wagon, he snarled, "Well, now, big man, we'll see how damned good you are."

Jimmy Blunt held back, waiting for a direction from Stanton, who shifted close to Blake. But Farner called out firmly, "Will you stop, Stanton? Durant doesn't mean to make trouble."

Stanton's face darkened. But, just as he was about to express his own decision on this matter, Blake, catching Schofield off-guard, stepped in behind the tall man and with one blow jolted the gun out of his hand. Before Jute Carney could fire a shot, Blake had Schofield's body in front of him and his own gun was in his hand.

"Carney, drop it! Blunt, keep out of it. Stanton, one more word of fight from you and by hell you'll get everything you ask for and more."

Farner moved angrily to the side and Ellen saw fear flood into Mike Stanton's face. Whatever doubts she might have had about her feelings towards Mike Stanton, they were settled at that moment. Jute Carney gave a sharp curse and worked his horse back, refusing to drop his gun. But he held his fire and it was Art Schofield who bellowed: "Damn you, Jute, do you want me killed? Do as he says!" Jute Carney still worked his horse back. Then Mike Stanton said tightly, "Jute, do it. Durant wins this round, too. But his time's coming."

"My time is now, Stanton," Blake told the wagon boss. "Twice now your scum have tried to cut me down. Twice they've failed. But I don't give a damn about that; I'm interested only in getting another matter settled."

Blake pushed Schofield away and when Schofield bent down to retrieve his gun, Blake kicked him in the seat of the pants and sent him sprawling. Out of the corner of his eye Blake saw Ellen Farner smiling at that. He moved across to her father, saying:

"Well, what's it to be?"

"We'll take them on, Durant, but only as long as the woman keeps her word and makes no trouble among us. The first sign that she intends otherwise and we'll kick her out."

Blake nodded his thanks, then pulled Sundown to him and swung into the saddle.

But Stanton, who had noticed Lil for the first time, snapped, "What the hell is this, Farner? You know this woman, don't you?"

"Damn saloon tramp," growled Schofield, but Lil gave him such a venomous look that he backed away and said no more.

"I don't care much what she was before, Stanton," Farner said firmly. "All of us have things in our past that we'd rather hide. But I won't be a party to leaving her and a near-dead man out here to die. She can travel with me and I'll be responsible for both of them."

Ellen saw Lil's gaze lift to her. Coloring a little, she said, "We can make a bed for the man in the back."

Rick Trice exploded, "Ellen, you don't know what you're saying. Why, this woman—"

"This woman is in trouble, Rick Trice. Now please let's have no more of it."

Blake saw a change come into Lil's face. He said, "I think you'll be all right here."

Lil did no more than nod, her eyes fixed on Ellen Farner. Blake drew his horse back and watched Carney closely. When he reached the edge of the creek he put Sundown into a run.

But no sooner had the black stallion begun to gallop than Carney jerked up his gun and punched off two shots as Farner's voice rose in protest. Moments later Blake Durant was out of sight.

CHAPTER FIVE
Decision at Turn Creek

For two days Blake Durant followed the tracks of three riders. They never moved far from the wagon train's route, but he didn't sight them, mainly because he was careful to mask his own movements.

On the morning of the third day after leaving Lil and Croft with the Farner family, Blake came upon a camp that clearly showed the presence of four men. He checked and rechecked the signs until finally he discovered the tracks of one horse heading back in the direction of the wagon train. Losing the trail in shale country, he cut south. When he picked up the trail of the first three riders, he knew that his earlier suspicions about this wagon trek were correct. Somehow Dan Rinald knew the exact movements of the wagon train and was always camped where he could keep his eye on them, yet he hadn't made an attack. Blake wondered if this was because he was at poor strength now, with only two riders.

The mystery of the fourth man didn't puzzle him for long. Now he began to put things together, right from the first day out of Lusc. Stanton had from the beginning been opposed to having him along, although Blake couldn't see how another gun hand would be a load for any wagon outfit to carry, especially as hostiles like Dan Rinald and his outfit were rumored to be out in front of them.

Blake had spoken against Stanton taking this trail into the heart of Colonel Howie's territory, So Stanton had reason to be sour on him. But sour enough to send three men to kill him? Blake didn't think so.

So there was something else behind it. His mind turned back to the visitor at Rinald's last camp, a rider who had come in the night and left in the night, heading back to Farner's wagon train. Blake now remembered other times when Schofield, Blunt and Carney had been missing, presumably to check out the trail ahead and track down Rinald. It struck him as extremely strange that he himself had locked horns with Dan Rinald twice now, and Croft and Lil Anderson also, but Stanton's men hadn't sighted them.

Blake turned Sundown into a creek and let him water. Stretching his legs, he moved among the tall trees, wondering why people couldn't leave him alone. There were times when the past came back with all its heartbreak, and at those times he would just ride off and lose himself. But there was always someone putting demands on him.

Returning to Sundown, he swung into the saddle. High on the ridge line in front of him, he caught the glint of sunlight on metal. Blake immediately brought Sundown back into the shadows and held him still. Minutes later he saw three riders in single file. They crossed an open space and put their horses to the run, heading east. Soon they were out of sight. Blake, studying the terrain between himself and the trio, realized that it would take him a good half hour to negotiate the climb.

He pulled his range coat about his wide shoulders and heeled Sundown into a gallop. He went straight down the line of the creek in the direction of the route the wagon train would have to take to get to these lush valleys. He rode hard, not sparing the powerful horse, and Sundown pounded across the country, head high, mane flowing, every muscle tuned for speed and distance.

Fifteen minutes later Blake drew rein at a bend in the river. The wagon train had struck camp a mile or so away, but in one glance he saw that the wagons were too strung out, too vulnerable to attack from any of three directions. There was no movement anywhere among the wagons and the morning fires had not yet been lit. Blake pulled Sundown to a walk and threaded his way through the river bank trees until he sighted Roland Farner's wagon at the bank's edge, a long distance from the other wagons. Apparently Farner had decided to keep Lil away from the others.

Stepping down from the stallion, Blake walked to the wagon. He hitched Sundown and called quietly, "Farner?"

There was movement inside the wagon and then Lil poked her head out. "Blake," she said, excitement in her voice. But then she frowned and her voice lowered. "You shouldn't be here, Blake. Stanton's done a power of talking against you. They know you killed a man in Cheyenne and another in Twinkle Creek. He's turned the most tolerant of these people against you and he even has them wondering if you're linked up with Rinald. I tried to speak up on your behalf but of course it didn't do any good at all."

"Naturally," Blake said. Then: "Where's Farner?"

"He sleeps with the Watson family."

"And his daughter?"

"She's here with me."

"I've got to speak to her."

Suddenly Lil drew aside and Ellen pushed past her. Too late, she pulled her blouse across her bosom. Blake saw color rise in her cheeks as she realized he'd seen her naked breasts.

Blake said, "Can you get your father here in a hurry? It's important."

Ellen looked worried. "Mr. Durant, you shouldn't be here. Mike Stanton has turned everybody against you. His men are ready to shoot you down on sight."

"That's a risk I have to take, Miss Farner. Please get your father. And don't tell anyone else about my being here."

Ellen buttoned up her blouse, her back to him. Then she turned and said, "Why must you always take risks?"

"Because, ma'am, I think this outfit is going to be attacked. Dan Rinald is coming and the way things look here he can be through this camp and out of it before any of you people can stop him. Now will you hurry, girl?"

Ellen jerked upright, her mouth opening. "Girl?" she threw at him, annoyed. "Mr. Durant, I've driven this wagon halfway across the country. I've done my chores as well and perhaps better than the older women. I've taken my turn with the children and I've even—"

"You've done fine, Ellen," Durant said, putting warmth into his voice. "But hurry, please. Every minute counts."

Ellen gave him no more argument. She stepped down from the wagon and, straightening her skirt as she went, hurried across the compound. Two women were fussing at making a fire when she ran past but Ellen took no notice of them nor did she return their greetings. She returned two minutes later with a sleepy-eyed, scowling Roland Farner.

Farner stopped in front of Blake, and growled, "What now, Durant? Ellen came to me with some ridiculous story that Dan Rinald and his outlaws are about to raid us. Do you intend to keep stirring up worry in this camp?"

"Somebody has to," Blake said hotly. "Farner, take a look at this camp. Were you responsible for laying it out?" Farner turned and looked. "What's wrong with it?"

"If attacked from west, south or north, this outfit wouldn't stand a chance against anybody. Rinald might only have two men to help him, but he could take this camp apart before you fools got on your feet."

Farner muttered an oath and eased Ellen away. Then he threw a sour look at Lil and snapped, "Durant, we've been told a lot more about you and I don't like any of it. For one thing, you've killed many men. For my money, you take too much interest in the affairs of this camp. Now why don't you take your suspicions elsewhere and leave us be? And keep your distance from my daughter."

Ellen gasped. But Blake merely shrugged. "Okay, Farner, it's your neck. I'll leave you be."

"I'd appreciate that, Durant."

Blake, furious, turned on his heel. He was walking to his horse when a gunshot ripped the morning's quiet. A woman at the fire jumped up and screamed. The other woman bumped into her before she broke into a run. Within seconds the whole compound echoed with the sound of thundering hoofs and gunfire. One wagon burst into flames as a bullet struck a kerosene lantern and more screams and shouts rose to fill the camp. Lil Anderson pulled Ellen back towards the wagon and forced her to take cover. Roland Farner reached up and pulled his rifle from under the wagon seat. Turning to Durant he said:

"By hell, Durant, looks like you're right!"

"Fight from here," Blake told him. "You've got no chance of linking up with the others. I'll do what I can to organize them."

"You'll do nothing, mister," Farner swore at him, then he was running. Two riders bore down on Farner. Blake swung onto Sundown and sent him running between Farner and the riders. They saw him coming and wheeled away, then ran their mounts through the scattered wagons. The burning wagon was being pushed clear of a neighbor's rig by four men who went to ground in the path of the two riders. Guns blasted and one of the farmers cried out in pain.

Blake sent Sundown after them, his gun bucking. But they managed to use the wagons for cover and then they linked up with a third rider. Blake continued after them and was surprised to see the three riders turn their horses and head for the creek. Blake drew rein as men ran from the wagons, guns at the ready. Then Blake heard his name called. He wheeled Sundown around and saw Mike Stanton coming on the run. Directly behind Stanton were Schofield and Blunt.

Stanton, his Colt on Blake, said, "Okay, Durant, drop that gun or I'll shoot you where you sit."

Schofield, grinning in triumph, closed in on Blake's right. Before Blake could answer Stanton, Schofield rose in his saddle and swung his gun down hard on the side of Blake's head. He pitched forward in the saddle and felt himself falling. Sundown whinnied as Blake hit the ground on his shoulder. He tasted blood before he passed out.

Roland Farner stood in front of the circle of farmers and said tightly, "Durant woke me just before the attack, Stanton. He gave me warning about the raid and by hell I won't see him manhandled because of that."

Mike Stanton smiled. "How long before the raid, Farner? A minute maybe? Time enough to establish an alibi for himself and get himself in good standing with you. Don't be a fool man! Durant's a killer. He tried all along to make trouble here, to turn you men against me. He lied about the trail. He lied about me." Stanton shook his head. "No, Farner, I think you've been taken in, but I don't hold that against you. Durant is a pretty cunning customer. You can see his shrewdness now. He came to give you warning in case the attack failed, which it did because we're dealing with cowardly scum—and that includes him. I'll tell you what I think of our friend here, Farner. Durant is working with Rinald and his outfit. He's in cahoots with them right down the line, and just as soon as I can establish the truth of that, I'll have him hanged."

Farner pulled thoughtfully at his lip, then he shook his head stubbornly. "What about the three Rinald men Durant shot in the hills, Stanton? How do you explain that?" Stanton chuckled and shook his head again. "Farner, you're more confused than I thought you were. What three men? Who's seen any dead men? Whose word do we have that Durant did this? Only his own and that saloon tramp's. If I'm wrong about her being a liar and a slut, then a lot of people in Lusc were wrong about her, too. What's she doing out here in the wilderness anyhow?"

Roland Farner had no answers. He was silent for a moment, aware that men behind him were beginning to be swayed by Stanton.

Finally, Farner said: "She said she was heading west, and she admitted that she knew Rinald and that he has pestered her for years."

"She knew him all right," Stanton said. "Damn right she did. Why not admit that in case somebody makes trouble later? Who else is there now on Durant's side? A simpleton, the idiot companion of a man who was hanged for robbery." Stanton rocked back on his heels and laughed scornfully. "Now I ask you, Roland, whose side are you on? Are you with these people, a killer, a saloon tramp and a simpleton? Or are you on the side of the men in this camp? To hell with Rinald! You saw what happened when he tried to come to grips with us. First sign of fight and he took to his heels."

"With Durant after him," Farner said quietly, but there wasn't much conviction in his voice now.

Stanton threw his hands in the air. "Sure! We all saw our big hero Durant give chase to them. But not one of their bullets hit him, and he was only one man against three. And not one bullet hit him in that fight he told about. Come now, Roland, you're not a complete fool. And don't ask me to be one. We'll keep Durant trussed up where I can watch him. Just as soon as we have time, we'll give him a fair trial. Then by hell we'll hang him. I guess you know that a friend of yours was killed by those cowardly scum this morning."

Mike Stanton motioned for Schofield and Blunt to take Blake Durant into a wagon. As soon as Durant, still unconscious, had been dragged off, Roland Farner looked around at his friends.

When they avoided his gaze, he drew in a deep sigh and returned to his wagon.

Lil Anderson and Ellen were anxiously awaiting his return. Noting his slumped shoulders and heavy walk, Lil asked anxiously, "What do they mean to do?"

"Hold Durant till later. He'll get a fair trial."

"For doing what?" she exploded.

"Plenty of charges have been laid against his name."

Lil went to move past him but he stopped her with a hand on her arm. He looked into her anger-filled face and said tightly:

"You can't help him, Miss Anderson. You can only make it worse for him."

"But why, Pa?" Ellen demanded to know. "What did Mr. Durant do but warn us?"

Farner shook his head. "It's a complicated business. I want you both to leave the matter to me. I must have time to think. When I've done that I'll discuss the matter with you both."

"And by then Stanton will have killed Durant," Lil said. "I know his damned kind—pompous, overbearing, a conceited dude! He doesn't fool me one spit with his fancy manners and fine clothes. His kind I really know about, believe you me."

Farner eyed her heavily. "Nevertheless, Miss Anderson, while you ride along with us you'll do as I say. I suggest that you worry about Croft and forget all about our friend Durant for the moment."

Lil tightened her mouth and glared defiantly at him. But when Farner went to the front of the wagon to shackle the horses, she drew in a sigh. Ellen, watching her, said:

"He means a lot to you, doesn't he, Miss Anderson?"

Lil glanced at her, a slight pucker coming to her brow. She guessed she was ten years older than Ellen. From the first she'd felt jealousy towards the girl. But Ellen had proved to be a great deal more mature and understanding than most women she'd met. The girl had gone out of her way to be friendly. Lil decided now that she liked her. She said:

"Blake Durant is a real man, Ellen, and nobody will ever be able to convince me otherwise. And as for being a coward, well, that's one thing he is definitely not. He walked into the gunfire of three killers to save my life and Croft's. So he means a lot to me, yes, and if I get my way he'll mean a hell of a lot more."

Lil walked off. Ellen listened to her father working the horses into the shafts. Usually she helped him with that chore, but this morning she stood and looked across the camp at Mike Stanton's wagon. She was confused about a lot of things and she was deeply worried about Blake Durant.

CHAPTER SIX
A Need for Changes

Lil Anderson waited for the wagons to get under way before she went to Croft's side. For three days now the giant's condition had been slowly improving. But his face was still gray and his breathing slow and labored.

Lil handed him a water canteen. "How do you feel?"

Croft smiled at her and drank. Handing the canteen back, he looked vacantly through the canvas flap. "Green," he muttered.

"Yes, everything's green, Croft. The worst of it is over, so they tell me."

Lil settled back and tidied her hair. She tried to act casual, but not for a moment did she take her eyes off the big man. Croft was smiling.

Finally Lil said, "They have Mr. Durant tied up, Croft." His head turned slowly and he looked puzzled.

"You remember Mr. Durant, don't you?"

Croft thought deeply about this and then shook his head. Lil leaned closer to him and spoke above the grind of the wheels.

"Croft, we rode into the hills, you and me. We made camp and you built a good fire. Then some men attacked us and grabbed me and beat you up. They took our horses and our food."

Croft's brow rutted deeper. He seemed to be making a tremendous effort to comprehend.

Lil continued impatiently, "Damn you, don't you know anything? You carried me away and then we ran into Mr. Durant. He helped us, gave us food and water and brought us to the wagons."

Croft dropped his head to one side and his hands rose to feel at the bandages on his chest. "The wagons," he mumbled.

"But before we came here we were attacked again. You killed a man with your bare hands. He was after me. He wanted to hurt me."

Croft lifted his head suddenly and his eyes were bright with anger. His fingers closed into his broad palms and his breathing became more rapid.

Excited, Lil went on, "Then you do remember. You must! Mr. Durant brought us here and we've been well looked after. Their doctor stitched up your wounds and said you'd be all right. But Mr. Durant won't be all right unless somebody helps him. He saved our lives. He was good to us. He likes you, Croft, and you like him."

"Durant?" The name was scarcely audible from Croft's bruised lips. He took his gaze from Lil Anderson and he studied the country outside again. "Durant?" he mumbled.

"A big man with a hide coat. He gave me the coat when my dress was torn. He had a big horse, a big black horse so beautiful that you were always stroking it. You loved his horse and the horse liked you, Croft."

Lil looked hopefully at him. Suddenly Croft smiled.

"The big horse," he muttered.

"Yes," Lil said eagerly. "Now—do you remember Mr. Durant?"

Croft looked into her eyes. After a long moment he nodded. "Durant," he said.

Lil took his bruised hands in her own. "Croft, Mr. Durant is a friend of ours. He saved our lives and he's been very good to me. But right now he's tied up. They mean to kill him."

Croft swayed back from her and shook his big head. Locks of his hair, always unruly despite Lil's frequent attempts to tidy it up, fell over his lined brow.

"Yes, Croft, it's true. I wouldn't lie to you, would I?" Lil pulled back the canvas flap and pointed to a wagon leading the second line of strung-out wagons across the grasslands.

"There, in that wagon with other men I hate, Croft. They have Mr. Durant and they mean to kill him."

Croft drew in a quick breath and tried to rise. But Lil pushed him back and, more excited now, said, "Not now. Later. When I tell you, go across there and get him free. But be careful. There are men with guns there. They'll try to stop you."

Croft shook his shaggy head. "No," he said with such firmness that Lil knew he did, in his own simple way, understand. How he was going to get past the guards she did not know, but if he had some strength left then she could see nothing wrong in his using that strength to help Blake Durant. Nothing else mattered to Lil now. If she could get Durant free, he would be deeply obligated to her. Perhaps that obligation would make him forget a lot of other things.

Patting Croft on the head, she told him to lie still and then she climbed through the canvas flap to join Ellen. The younger woman, her face bathed in perspiration, gave her a tired smile and said:

"I wonder how much farther we have to go? You'd think the horses would drop, just plodding on, day after day, mile after mile."

Lil just nodded. Her eyes were sparkling as she looked eagerly about. Her sudden change of manner made Ellen remark:

"You seem to be all sparked up, Miss Anderson. Is it Croft?"

"Croft?" Lil said, unable to hide the alarm in her voice.

"Yes. Is he better?"

"Oh. Yes, he's a lot better. In fact, I think that in a day or so he'll be on his feet."

"You think a great deal of him, don't you?"

Lil shrugged. "He's been good to me. He'd die for me. I can't forget that. But at times it's like having a weight around your neck. He doesn't talk much, no more than a mumble. And when he likes something he goes into a trance. You can't share anything with him." Lil wiped her hair back with a tired gesture, the previous excitement drained out of her already by the dust and the heat. "It's like having a piece of timber about," she said finally.

Ellen held the reins high as the horses negotiated a downgrade. The wagon pitched badly to one side but then Ellen hit the horses into a faster stride and the wagon bounced out of some deep ruts, righted itself and they went on. Releasing her hold on the side of the wagon Lil said with relief:

"You'll make it out here. You'll find your place. Have you a man?"

Color flooded into Ellen's face and Lil laughed at her discomfort.

"You have then, Ellen. I'm glad. A woman needs a man. I haven't always thought that way. There have been times even when I've thought of getting a gun and shooting down every one of their breed I could find." She smiled again. "But then the loneliness sets in ... and the want."

"The want?" Ellen asked.

Lil studied her thoughtfully for a moment before she patted her thigh. "That will come to you in time, although I'm surprised it hasn't stirred inside you yet. You're very beautiful, enough to set a town of men barking. Just remember to select your man carefully. Don't rush into a tie-up with one of them just for the sake of ... well, just for the sake of that 'want' I mentioned. Would you like me to take a turn with the reins?"

Ellen shook her head. "No, Pa will relieve me at noon. He doesn't like anybody else handling the team but me. I guess when a wagon is practically all a man has, he must be careful with it."

Lil nodded to signify that she understood and then she leaned back. Each bone-jolting mile was taking her closer to the next camp. And when they struck that, Croft would make his move. Then Blake Durant would be free. Settled back, Lil Anderson wondered who Ellen Farner's man could be.

84

But Ellen Farner thought of only one man. Blake Durant.

* * *

"What the hell are we gonna do with him now?" Art Schofield asked sourly, jerking a hand at Blake Durant. They had camped an hour ago and after a meal and a drink, Blunt, Carney and Schofield were playing cards. The breeze from the river was cool and sounds from the other wagons drifted to them.

"Mike'll work it out," Jimmy Blunt said. "He always does, doesn't he?"

"Could've shot Durant's stinkin' guts out back there. Should've when I had the chance," Carney growled. "But no matter, he's mine in the end, make no mistake about that."

Blunt dealt the cards and Carney, after a brief inspection of his hand, tossed the pasteboards angrily into the center of the box they were using as a table. "You'd give hog feed to your kids, Blunt. Ain't you ever learned to deal anything above a ten?"

"Only to myself," Blunt said and spread his cards flat on the box top. "Buyin', Art?"

Art Schofleld went on studying his cards for a moment before he eyed Blunt distrustfully. As always, Blunt's face was expressionless and gave away nothing. Schofield tossed two cards down and asked for two more.

When he had them he waited for Blunt to discard. Blunt shuffled his cards and held Schofield's gaze until Schofield said impatiently, "Well, Jimmy, what are you buyin'?"

"I'm happy with what I've got, Art. Bet as you like."

Schofield sat back, his face darkening, his stare fixed on Jimmy Blunt's big face. Bruises were dotted about Blunt's cheeks and a huge welt showed on the side of his jaw. But he had recovered better than any of them from the punishment meted out by Blake Durant.

Schofield growled, "You ain't buyin' again, Jimmy? Strikes me that every time you deal things come out fine for you."

"That's the way it should be, Art. What was your bet?"

Schofield checked on Jute Carney who sat back with his hands on his thighs. Carney eyed him coolly. "Yeah, always when you deal, Jimmy. Maybe that ain't right, eh?"

Jimmy Blunt packed his cards together and placed them on the box top. He spread his big hands over them.

"Art, lately you've gotten to say some loco things. If I was you, I'd watch that. Could get you into a heap of trouble."

Schofield's lips peeled back and he sat upright, his jaw clenched hard. "I don't reckon trouble worries me much, Blunt. Not when I know where it's coming from and how big it is."

"Maybe it's too big for you," Blunt said, his hands shifting back and forth across the cards.

Jute Carney's eyes gleamed. "Maybe we'll have a little excitement going here."

"Shut up, damn you!" Schofield rasped. "This is between Blunt and me." Schofield leaned forward and held Blunt's look. "When you deal, things always come out just fine for yourself, Blunt. Yep. You always come out on top after you handle the cards. How come? Have you got a real cute answer for that?"

"Yeah, one answer," said Blunt and his hands lifted and reached for Art Schofield's throat.

But Schofield was ready for the move. He kicked himself back, and jumped to his feet in the one action. Jute Carney did nothing but grin.

Blunt, caught off-balance when he was unable to reach Art Schofield, rose slowly, his big body hunched forward, "Damn you, mister, lately you been giving me the sours. When we went for Durant out there, you kept right out of the firing line. You did a power of talking but you didn't lose much sweat. It was me and Jute who closed in and got hit, not you."

Blunt was standing tall now, his face black with anger. For a moment Jute Carney studied them both. Then he got to his feet and his hand clamped on his gun butt.

He said, "No matter how it goes, I'm down the middle. You remember it, both of you. I ain't takin' sides, not yet."

The two men took no notice of him. Carney moved to the end of the wagon, where relief from the afternoon's heat came in the form of a cool wind from the creek. Carney smiled and waited.

"So, Art?" Blunt said challengingly.

Art Schofield licked at his lips. His breathing was fast and loud. "I ain't scared of you, Blunt. I can take you."

"Maybe you can, Art. You just keep sayin' what you just said and you're gonna get your chance. You're a bad loser, Art, but more than that you're a *born* loser."

Schofield's mouth opened, but before he could make more of the argument, Mike Stanton came riding in. He reined up. One look at the three of them and he knew there was trouble. He studied them all bleakly for a moment, then said, "What gives?"

All three turned to look at him and Jute Carney saw relief move into Schofield's face. Carney knew then whose side he'd be on should the feud grow into something bigger later on.

"Nothin' is wrong, Mike," he told Stanton. "Art and Jimmy were just circlin', lookin' for an opening. Hell, you might've stopped something that would've relaxed all of us. Been too damned monotonous and slow out here, ain't it?"

Stanton shifted his horse against Schofield and swore viciously. "Cards?" he barked. "Is that it? You at that again, Art?"

Art Schofield's lips came together tightly. His look hardened. "We're on free time, Mike," he said. "Our business."

Mike Stanton's face hardened. "Damn you! You ain't got no free time, not when you work for me! We got a good thing going for us, the best any of you damn scum will ever get within reach of. A whole new section of the country is there for the taking. There are fools to do our hard fighting and working. You gonna throw that away just over a damned argument with some cards?"

Schofield said nothing. Jimmy Blunt uncurled his fingers and wiped his big hands down his shirt front.

"It's over then," Stanton said. He eyed Schofield until the tall man nodded.

"Sure, over," Schofield grunted.

Stanton breathed a loud sigh of relief and came out of the saddle. He looked down to where the rest of the wagons had been run into a circle. Women were moving about, doing their chores and talking. The men were down at the creek watering the horses, cattle and oxen. Children were running riot through the wagons and under them, their shrill shouts spoiling the peace of the afternoon.

Stanton said: "Okay, everything's set. Farner'll get his tonight. Jute, I want you to stay close to Ellen, see that nothing happens to her. Jimmy, put that Anderson woman in her place, and I don't care what you have to do to her. Art, Croft's yours. Come morning I want Farner, that woman and that big, stupid ox out of the way. Durant won't be around either, so I reckon we can get on with the next part of the plan."

"How close is it?" Blunt asked.

"Two days of easy going. There's a big valley right in front with plenty of timber, good water, good grazing. These fools will stop dead in their tracks when they see it. We'll have them cutting timber and building before another three days are out. Then the rest will happen—as planned."

Jute Carney scratched at the side of his jaw and looked doubtful. When Stanton's look sought him out, he muttered, "Ain't it gonna be slow, Mike? I mean, hell, we got to wait for these farmers to build us a town. Be better to find one already made up, wouldn't it, and take it?"

"There's a ranch already made up, one of the best spreads west of the Platte and nobody to ask questions when we take it." Stanton was grinning confidently now, his handsome face bright with excitement.

The others, their argument forgotten for the moment, closed in. Blunt asked, "Howie country?"

Stanton nodded. "What else?"

Jute Carney looked confused. "If it's been that all along, why the damned delay? Why didn't we just push on and take over?"

"Because from what I hear Colonel Howie has a big outfit, sworn to fight for him, rough riders from way back who know no loyalty but to him. They're mostly drifters and army deserters, misfits on the move until they linked up with him. Howie gave them a place to set down roots, gave them freedom of a kind they never had before. They don't have to worry about the law, about nothing, just so they keep his empire for him. Twice a year he closes up the place, leaves a skeleton staff and takes his boys way across the border where they kick up their heels. But they always go back with him, so he's got to have something that those fellers want. And we'll have it—money, land, cattle, everything any of us ever dreamed of."

Jute Carney looked at Stanton's bright-eyed face and wondered how much dreaming Mike Stanton did. Plenty, he decided. But then Stanton's kind had always confused him. He followed them, letting them make their decisions, and often they made bad leaders. But maybe Stanton was different. As far as Jute Carney was concerned Stanton had this cleverly worked so far, his only mistakes coming when Durant got in their way.

But now Durant was finished. So was Farner, who always rallied the rest of the fools behind him. Without Farner, the others would be leaderless. Then suddenly Jute Carney got it.

"They'll do our fighting for us, Mike. Is that it?"

"Why shouldn't they? Especially when they have fine country for the asking and a damned cattleman's outfit tries to run them off. I've got it all planned, make no mistake about it. Just do what I said to do tonight and leave the rest to me."

Stanton's face hardened again and he checked on Schofield and Blunt in turn. "No more of that argument, right?" Both men shook their heads. Mike Stanton, after a look towards the Farner wagon where Ellen was getting the evening meal together, made his way down to her.

Pulling his horse up just short of her, Stanton removed his hat and bowed from the saddle. "Ellen, in two days' time, I'm going to show you the best slice of country you ever laid your eyes on. I've just ridden ahead and checked it out. I guess I could have staked my right to whatever section I wanted for myself, but I decided that everybody here gets a fair chance to lay his claim."

Ellen rose, smoothing her skirt. Knowing that this man was holding Blake Durant prisoner, she couldn't bring herself to show any enthusiasm over his visit.

"That's fine, Mr. Stanton," she said. "Everybody will be relieved. It's been such a long trip and very difficult at times."

"Well, it's nearly over," Stanton said, in no way put off by her reserved manner. His gaze ran down her body. Soon she would be his. An empire would be his. And nobody would be able to stop him.

He said, "You'll find out that all the hardship has been worth it. I've brought you to the promised land, just as I said I would. We've had our problems but I think they are all behind us."

"What about Mr. Durant?" Ellen asked.

Stanton's lips tightened just a little, but then he was smiling again. "I haven't decided what to do with him. Perhaps when Durant realizes everything I have done is for the good of this outfit, his manner towards me will change. Men like him would be handy when the time comes to carve out a township. I don't like the man, but I must admit he has some qualities I admire."

Ellen was completely taken aback by Stanton's change of attitude. "You mean that if Mr. Durant changes his ways, you'll set him free?"

Stanton rose in the saddle, beaming. "Wait until you see the valley I've just seen, Ellen. On each side high mountain ridges shut it in and deep gorges and ravines cut back into those ridges. There are green meadows and tumbling waterfalls and all the hills around are timbered to their crests. It's beautiful country, the kind that makes all thoughts of violence leave a man's head. But, about Durant ... well, I'm not making a decision just yet. However, I don't want to start a new life, with people I've come to respect, admire and ... and love, with blood on my hands."

Ellen moved quickly towards him. "Oh, Mike, that's wonderful news. I just know the others will thank you for this. Mr. Durant did come to alert us to the attack from Dan Rinald. But, as we all know now, we don't have to worry about Dan Rinald, although Mr. Durant could not have known how cowardly the outlaw is. I'm so happy."

Stanton smiled down at her. "It's good to see you happy, Ellen. It's how I always want to see you. I'd spend my whole life making sure of that ... if you'll let me."

Ellen drew away and looked down at her hands. She managed to keep the smile on her face but there was little warmth in it.

Stanton came down from the big white mare, hitched the reins loosely over the side of the wagon and approached her. His face was suddenly serious.

"Ellen, you're a grown woman, the most beautiful I've ever seen. In the beginning, when we started this trek, I had visions of a home out here someplace ... a home and a family. I admit now in all humility that I thought of you as part of my family, but I didn't dare hope it would ever be so. Then, all during the crossing, I've been unable to think of anything else. Even when work was at its hardest and demands on me came from every quarter, I've always had the consolation that I might have a chance with you."

Seeing Ellen stiffen, Stanton moved back and looked about him.

"It'll take time, I know. There is much to be done. But I want you to think seriously about marrying me. I also want you to think of what I've done and how I've done it— for the good of all concerned, not just for myself. There has been friction and trouble, but it's over. Now each of us must plan ahead. This is a wilderness we've come to and we must stick together. There will be good times and bad and we'll all need each other, somebody to lean on. But this is no country for the likes of Blake Durant, Ellen. His kind won't stay in one place; they can't put down roots. But you're farmer stock. Though it might sound strange to you, I'm farmer stock, too. I want a home and fields to work and cattle to run."

Stanton drew the mare towards him. Ellen's face was red with embarrassment as his hungry eyes took in her body. She remembered the words of Lil Anderson: "There is a want in every woman."

Stepping back into the saddle, Stanton refitted his hat to his head and smiled. "There's plenty of time, Ellen. I'm impatient where you're concerned, but I can wait. I will wait. Just give me a fair hearing and you'll find I can make you happy."

Stanton turned the horse and rode away. Ellen felt her legs trembling. She made fists of her hands and bit at her bottom lip. She couldn't deny the fact that his appraisal of her body had excited her. There were emotions stirring inside her that she had never experienced before. She returned to the fire and put on dry tinder, and knelt there, not worrying about the smoke lifting past her face.

Her mind returned to the day Blake Durant had appeared on the ridgeline, sitting on his black stallion. It was a sight she would never forget, because that was when Ellen Farner felt what Lil Anderson said only grown women could experience.

Now she knew. And she was grateful to Mike Stanton for telling her so definitely. Ellen Farner was in love with Blake Durant.

CHAPTER SEVEN
Break Out!

Lil put a restraining grip on Croft's big arm. When he looked down on her, she asked, "Do you know what to do?"

The giant nodded.

"Are you sure?"

Croft grunted and made to move away. But Lil stopped him again. Her eyes were clouded with tears when she said, "You be careful. Mr. Durant is a friend who needs your help, but you must be very careful. You'll fail if you make a mistake."

Croft worked his huge shoulders. Lil knew he must be in pain but the big man gave no sign of it. In fact, a smile moved across his bruised lips.

"Go up behind the wagon," she said. "There are three of them there. Do what you have to do to get Mr. Durant free, then hurry back."

Croft walked away slowly. The daylight was fast diminishing and already Mike Stanton's wagon was just a blurred outline against the backdrop of tall trees along the riverbank. Croft had gone only a dozen or so paces when Roland Farner walked up from the creek past the circle of farmers' wagons. When he saw Croft on his feet, he stopped in surprise.

Then, as he saw Croft's hands bunched at his sides and his look fixed on Stanton's wagon, Roland Farner knew something was wrong.

"Croft!"

The giant halted and looked at him. In the last few days Farner had taken his turn feeding Croft and changing his bandages. Recognition of the farmer came into Croft's eyes, but then Lil came running towards him. Farner, certain now that the woman was up to something, hurried forward. He arrived in time to hear Lil urge Croft, "Go on. Nobody will stop you. Hurry."

Farner snapped, "Now, wait a minute! I told you when you came here that I'm responsible for everything you do in this camp. I want to know exactly what's going on."

"Nothing's going on," Lil lied. "Why don't you go polish Stanton's boots if you've got nothing better to do than check up on me and Croft? I hear you've changed sides again."

Farner's lips tightened and his stare was severe. "I've not changed sides at all, young woman, although it's none of your business if I have. Now what in blazes are you up to? No good, by the look of him."

"They mean to kill Blake Durant," Lil said. "And I aim to stop them. I know nobody else here will help me, not even your daughter since Stanton has filled her head with lies, too. Can't any of you see what's going on? Stanton has fooled the lot of you."

Farner regarded her angrily for a long moment before he
said to Croft, "Go back to the wagon. You're in no condition
to be moving about."

Lil glared at Farner as Ellen approached. Croft, who
hadn't moved from the moment he saw Farner, looked only
at Lil, his face slack, his eyes almost vacant.

"He won't listen to you, Farner," Lil said. "He does my
bidding. Try to stop him and you'll regret it, I promise you."

"Why you—!" Farner grasped her arm and Ellen cried out
for her father to stop. Lil, seeing Croft turning to them, let out
a cry of pain and broke free of Farner. When he reached for
her again, she beat at his chest with both hands. Ellen joined
in, trying to separate them, and Croft lumbered forward.
Grabbing Farner by the shoulder, he applied pressure that
made Farner double over in pain. Ellen, shocked by the
violence of the big man, rushed at him. Croft brushed her
aside and when she went sprawling, he looked down at her,
his mouth open. Farner staggered to his feet, raced back
to the wagon and grabbed his rifle from under the seat. Lil,
completely composed again, pulled Croft about and pointed
to Farner. "Stop him," she cried out.

Croft hesitated, then Lil pushed him and he lumbered
away. Farner saw him coming and jerked the rifle up. Croft,
clearly unable to work matters out for himself, swept his arm
across the side of Farner's head and sent him staggering
away, the rifle flying from his grip. Ellen jumped to her feet.
Dodging Croft, she hurried to her father's side.

Farner had not moved after falling. Lil, seeing this, sent Croft off, saying, "Be careful now."

The big man looked at Stanton's wagon again and his face returned to its earlier expression, his eyes staring, his features tight and his hands clenched at his sides.

Lil breathed a sigh of relief. Ellen, at her father's side, lifted his head into her lap and glared up at Lil. "What are you trying to do?" she demanded to know. "We befriended you. Is this the thanks we get for that?"

"There are bigger issues at stake, Ellen," Lil told her. "You must trust in me."

"Trust you?" Ellen shouted up at her. "After you turned that—that animal onto my father."

"There's something that must be done, girl," Lil said. "I'm grateful for your past help and friendship. Your father isn't badly hurt; Croft likes him and wouldn't hurt him in any way. I'll be leaving straight away."

Lil watched Croft closing in on Mike Stanton's wagon. When she saw him disappear behind the back of the wagon she rushed back to Farner's wagon and took the bundle of clothes Ellen had collected for her from the camp women.

* * *

Near the wagon, Art Schofield sat hunched forward on a box whittling at a stick with a long-bladed knife. Across from him Jute Carney was oiling his gun.

Jimmy Blunt, perched on the driving seat, stared moodily into the distance.

Croft walked straight up behind Schofield, making no sound at all. He looked curiously at them for a long moment before Schofield began to turn, sensing somebody behind him. When he saw the huge mountain of a man there with fists clenched, Schofield jumped off the box in alarm and grabbed at his gun.

"Jimmy! Jute!" he called out anxiously. Jute Carney looked up. When he saw Croft, blood rushed into his pinched face. He clamped his gun chamber closed and leveled the gun on Croft. Too late he realized he had emptied the gun to oil it. He dug bullets out of his belt while Blunt, jumping down from the wagon seat, landed heavily at his side and swept them away. Croft moved towards Schofield, looking into the man's mean eyes and not seeing the knife. Schofield, cornered against the wagon side after backing away from Croft, held the knife by the blade in throwing position. Then he hurled it. The knife entered Croft's shoulder He gave a grunt and pulled it free, then he broke the blade across his knee. As blood poured from his shoulder wound, he grasped Schofield by the arms, lifted him over his head and hurled him at Carney and Blunt.

Blake Durant watched anxiously from the wagon. He was tied so tightly that his arms and chest were numb. He squirmed helplessly in the bonds and cursed. He could do nothing but watch.

Blunt had his gun out now. He ducked as Schofield's body came flying at him. As he did so, panic-stricken Carney brushed past him. Blunt heard a sickening thud as Schofield's head cracked against the side of the wagon.

Then Carney shouted, "Okay, Jimmy, let's take him."

Blunt aimed carefully as Croft lumbered towards him. His gun bucked and the bullet thumped into Croft's chest. The giant came to a halt, his big face twisting in pain. But a moment later he drew in a breath and came on. Blunt gaped. Carney fired off three shots, all of which plowed into Croft, sending him reeling to the side. Blunt put his second shot into Croft, but the big man refused to go down.

Croft had sighted Blake Durant and had seen the alarm in his friend's face. Durant was a friend, Durant had helped him. Durant had helped Miss Lil. These were the thoughts crowding the giant's head as he moved towards Blunt again. Jimmy Blunt backed away, almost paralyzed with shock at the sight of this indestructible giant. Jute Carney, cursing viciously, circled, keeping his distance from Croft. He kept pumping off shots but the light was bad near the wagon and he wasn't sure if the bullets were hitting home or not.

Then Croft dropped on his knees beside Blake Durant and pushed the end of the broken knife into Blake's roped hands. He looked at Blake for a long, searching moment, then another bullet hit him in the middle of the back. Croft staggered to his feet and swung about. Jute Carney, his gun empty, moved away.

Jimmy Blunt, who had discovered in a brief examination that Art Schofield's neck was broken and his skull smashed, stopped and planted his feet solidly. As Croft came slowly and painfully towards him, Blunt said:

"You've got to be dead, big man ... got to be!"

He triggered another three shots which tore into Croft. The giant's body shook, then his knees doubled up under him and he pitched forward, onto his face. He lay there, unmoving, his face buried in the dust.

Jute Carney sucked breath through his teeth. Jimmy Blunt, now that the threat of Croft was gone, wheeled about anxiously, and saw Blake Durant rise in the wagon. Blunt fired but the shot went wide. Then the hammer fell on an empty chamber. As Blunt and Jute Carney prodded bullets into their guns, Blake, after a quick sad look at the huge hulk of Croft, dropped from the wagon and slipped into the darkness.

Blake circled the camp and came up behind the Farner wagon. Crouched, he listened to the shouts as men investigated the shooting. Ellen Farner and her father were nowhere in sight. Lil ran through a group of farmers to Mike Stanton's wagon. Then Blake saw Stanton striding up from the creek. Stanton's fire was stirred and fresh wood thrown on. In the light of the flames which licked up high soon after, Blake saw Jimmy Blunt refilling his gun. Jute Carney stood beside him, gun leveled, his mean little eyes searching.

Blake freed Sundown from the river corral where all the horses had been put and, swinging up, sent the big black stallion running. As he crossed the creek, rifles cracked and slugs whined around him. But Blake Durant, nursing blistered and bloodied wrists, rode into the night.

* * *

Lil Anderson dropped down tearfully at Croft's side and tried to lift his big head from the dust. She was still trying when Carney stepped forward, planted a boot against her back and sent her sprawling over the dead man.

Lil gave no cry of alarm or pain. She clawed her way over the bloodied Croft and glared up at Carney. "Swine!"

Carney leveled his gun on her, but Ellen Farner cried out, "No! Don't shoot her! Don't!"

"Put down the gun," Roland Farner said. Farmers were backed up behind him, all of them gravely silent. Schofield's body had been dragged into the light of the fire and the mutilation done to his body was plain for all to see. Three women turned away, holding their hands to their mouths.

"Damn her!" Carney said. "That big man did just what she told him to! She sent him up here. He killed Art and would've torn the lot of us apart if we hadn't shot him down. What the hell do you think this is, Farner?"

"I think everybody should quieten down," Farner said tightly. "Blake Durant has escaped. Perhaps that's for the best. I doubt if he'll ever show his face again."

Ellen Farner looked at her father and said nothing. Then Mike Stanton hurried up and bustled his way into the circle. When he saw the bodies of Croft and Schofield, he barked, "What the hell happened?"

Jute Carney told him. Stanton turned on Roland Farner then.

"I thought you were going to keep an eye on that stupid mauler. Is this the way you run your affairs? Is it the best you can do with the authority I've given you?"

Roland Farner pressed his lips together. Then Lil rose from Croft's side and wiping his blood down the front of her dress, said defiantly, "If you want to blame somebody, Stanton, blame me. I arranged all this. Croft was going to die and he knew it. But he died getting a friend free of your clutches. So do what you like with me, and I'll spit in your eye as you do it."

Ellen saw Stanton's fists clench. She moved quickly to Lil's side and took one of her hands. She felt Croft's blood and shuddered. Lil looked curiously at her; then, seeing the anger in the faces of the men, she pushed Ellen away.

"I don't need you," Lil said. "You're like the rest of them, listening to Stanton's fine talk about what a great man he is, about what a grand trip this is and what wonderful opportunities await all of you. Well, I'll tell you something else."

Lil spun about and glared at the ring of men.

"I'll tell you all something. Blake Durant is no bad man, no matter what he's done in the past. He alone has traded bullets with Dan Rinald's outfit and if you think for one minute that Dan Rinald is a coward and won't fight to get what he wants, then you're all sadly mistaken and will pay for it in the long run."

Jute Carney stepped over Art Schofield's body and pulled Lil away from Ellen. He swung her about and pushed her at Mike Stanton.

"Are you takin' that, Mike?" Carney asked.

Stanton looked at the men and decided he had their backing, with the possible exception of Roland Farner. His gaze took in Ellen's grave face and he read pity for Lil Anderson in it.

He said, "Jute, you and Jimmy take this floozy outside camp. Leave her with only what she came with. There's water in abundance ahead and food if she knows where to get it and how. Move!"

Stanton turned his back on her and then Lil lunged and clawed at his neck. Stanton wheeled back just as Jute Carney got hold of Lil again. His fist smashed into Lil's face and sent her and Carney reeling.

"Get her to hell out of my sight!" Stanton roared. "Take her away before I give her everything she's ever asked for in her life!"

106

Lil struggled free of Carney and tried to scratch at his eyes. But Jimmy Blunt grabbed her and held her helpless.

Suddenly she stopped struggling. "I want to bury Croft," she said. "I don't care about the rest of it. I want to go some place and wash the stench of these wagons off my body. But I must bury my friend, the only true friend I've had in my life."

"Throw her out!" Stanton roared. "We'll bury Croft. And at the same time we'll bury Art Schofield, who's worked hard and long for this outfit and won't ever get his rewards now." Stanton moved among the men, adding, "I want all of you to be in attendance when we bury Art. I want you to pay homage to a man who sacrificed himself to give you your chance, a man who stood against a brute, an insane wild animal, and lost out."

Mike Stanton walked off with Lil's curses following him. But then Carney, bleeding from an ear and under his right eye, grabbed her and jostled her off. Jimmy Blunt, following slowly, kept himself between the camp men and Carney and held his gun at his side.

CHAPTER EIGHT
Secret Alliance

Blake Durant stopped Sundown a mile or so from the wagon train. He wanted to learn about Stanton's next move. With the death of Croft, he realized that few people back there interested him at all. But there was the strangely nagging thought that Ellen Farner, when he got to know her better, might prove to be important to him. Then there was the unfortunate Lil.

It was an hour after sunup when Blake saw the lone figure tramping along the creek's edge. Seeing it was a woman, Blake put Sundown into a run.

Nearing the creek he saw the woman sink to her knees, then she fell onto her face. Blake spurred Sundown to her. Lil Anderson lifted her bruised face in fear but when she recognized Blake she let out a cry of relief and reached out. Blake came off Sundown and she fainted. He lifted her into his arms and carried her to the creek's edge. He gently bathed the blood from her face and saw that she had a split lip. One eye was closed. Lil opened her eyes.

"What happened?" he asked. "Did Stanton do this?"

"He ordered it, Blake. That little sneak Carney dragged me out of camp. Blunt was with him."

"Blunt had a hand in it?" Blake asked.

"I don't know, Blake. All I remember was Carney grabbing me and telling Blunt to watch the trail. Then he hit me with his fist. When I tried to fight him off, he went crazy. He's a maniac. He just kept hitting me and hitting me until I passed out. I don't know what happened after that."

Lil began to sob, from exhaustion as much as anything else. Blake lifted her to her feet and she leaned against him, her hands on his shoulders. Blake eased her back.

"Easy now," he said. "Everything will be all right."

"Will it, Blake?" she asked, the hint of a smile working across her swollen lips. "Will you look after me from now on? I don't have Croft to worry about now. He's dead, poor fool. But I'm alive, Blake, and you're alive. Get me out of here. Don't let any of them touch me again."

Blake led her to Sundown and helped her into the saddle. He looked thoughtfully up the trail. He knew he'd gone a good five miles past the wagon camp before coming back this way to make his check.

"Let's go on, Blake," Lil said pleadingly. "They mean nothing to you. Stanton has the run of things and everybody hates you back there now. Stanton is using Schofield's death to keep them against you."

Blake wiped sweat from his brow and swung up behind her. Lil leaned back against him and Blake said roughly, "I've got something to do, people to see. When we get to the end of this ride, behave yourself."

"I will, Blake, I swear."

They rode out of the creek country and headed due west. For the rest of that day and during most of the night, Blake pushed Sundown hard. By sunup the powerful black was spent and Blake had to call a halt.

Leaning against a tree stump in shade a little later, Lil looked pleased with herself. Her eyes never left Blake Durant and the speculation in her gaze made him suddenly annoyed.

"What else do you want, Lil? I've defended you three times now and you've crowded my trail. All right, I'm a man and you're a woman. Believe you me that means nothing to me."

Lil's eyes brightened with anger. "You're not a piece of timber, Blake Durant. You're a man with a man's desires. I might not be a pretty picture right now, but I will be in time. So don't ride your high horse with me and scorn me as—as something filthy."

"Nobody scorns you, Lil. Just don't jump to conclusions. I have an important man to see tomorrow morning, and I want to see him on my terms, not on yours."

Lil shrugged, picked up a straw and poked her even white teeth with it. "Don't you ever want a woman, Blake?" she asked as Durant closed his eyes in search of rest.

Blake frowned at her. "Sure. I'm human."

She smiled. "It's a lonely place out here, Blake. I'm lonely and you're lonely and tomorrow there will be a crowd. Surely you want to get something settled before we ride in to see Colonel Howie, don't you?"

Blake's eyes narrowed. "How do you know I'm going to Howie's place?"

Lil looked uncomfortable for a moment, then she smiled again. "Who else could it be? There's been so much talk about him in this territory. You yourself told me a little about him, about how he's jealous of his empire and doesn't allow settlers near him. Add to that, Mr. Blake Durant, the fact that at no time were you really part of the wagon train, just somebody keeping pace with it. When the people began to annoy you, you stayed on. I've been wondering why."

Blake scrubbed a hand roughly along his sweating neck, then closed his eyes and said, "Get some sleep, Lil. The trip ahead is going to be as hard as it was crossing the desert. This is the last rough section before the good country begins."

"Before the colonel's country begins," Lil said.

Blake didn't reply. He knew Howie, having met him years ago when he'd retired from the army and was looking for pasture land so he could start a ranch. Word had come to Blake that Howie had made it at last, nearly in isolation.

Needing that kind of isolation himself, he had written to Howie and asked for a job. A letter from Howie had told him to come out.

Blake finally drifted off to sleep, worried about Lil Anderson. Taking her into Howie's stronghold could be the undoing of Howie's plans. As a woman among woman-starved men, Blake knew Lil would use all her wiles to make a way for herself.

He heard her moving and opened his eyes, but she had merely changed position and was curled up on the ground, using a tree root for a pillow.

* * *

Blake Durant stopped Sundown and admired the sight before him. As far as he could see, rolling, well-grassed prairie met the eye.

The sun was warm but a cool breeze came down a wide, slow-running river. The surrounding slopes were heavily timbered, giving shelter to a number of depressions that were like small valleys. In the middle of one of the larger hollows stood six buildings; a large ranch house, a bunkhouse, a cookhouse, and three barns standing in line. The corrals were big and were fenced straight, the rails gleaming white in the sunlight.

"My God!" exclaimed Lil Anderson. "Have you ever seen such a sight, Blake?"

"Nope. It's good country."

"Good? Why, it's no wonder the colonel came out here and settled and refused to leave. Any person who did otherwise would be out of his head. It's an empire all right, just as he said it was."

Blake pulled her about by the shoulder. *"As he said it was?"*

Lil bit her lip, clearly annoyed at herself for making the mistake. Then she lifted her head defiantly. "Yes, Mr. Durant, Colonel Howie told me all about this place. It was many years ago and I haven't forgotten. At that particular time he showed a deep interest in me."

Blake swore under his breath. He knew now the answer to the riddle of a woman like Lil heading west on her own, unprepared for the rigors of the trail, depending solely on a man who didn't understand what went on around him. What had she intended to do with Croft at the end of her journey?

"It may have helped to tell me," he said. "Might have saved a lot of time, too. Did Howie ask you to come out?"

Lil held his gaze evenly. "Yes. As I said, it was years ago, but he was serious and he told me to keep thinking about it. He's lonely, despite his attempts to appear a complete man."

Blake turned Sundown side-on to the breeze. The big stallion whinnied.

Then Lil slid down from the saddle and brushed at her dress. Looking up at Blake, she said, "Will you tell him about me?"

"Tell him what?"

"About my recent life. I—I've never lied to you about myself. I hoped that you could close your eyes to a lot of things and come to like me and want me. If you had just paid me one bit of attention, I wouldn't have insisted on you bringing me out here. The colonel is one thing and my future is another."

Blake understood now and he didn't like how it added up. This little schemer was always one step ahead of things, with an alternative. First there had been Croft, then himself, then the Farner family, and finally it was him again. In the end, if she got her way, it would be Colonel Howie.

Blake let Sundown walk and Lil moved along at the horse's side, one hand on the saddlehorn. They turned through the big white gate which bore the brand of the Colonel Howie ranch: C.H. Blake had just closed the gate when four riders burst up from a hollow. All four held guns.

Blake said quietly, "Let me handle this."

But Lil didn't seem in the least worried. In fact, she wore a smile that had just enough invitation in it to encourage the four riders to keep their guns on Blake Durant instead of her.

Blake said, "Easy, boys! I'm not an intruder."

"No, mister?" said a lean, red-headed youth with battle
scars on his jaw and under his right eye. He turned to Lil,
then let his gaze sweep up and down her body before his
attention returned to Blake. "When you come ridin' in through
the colonel's gate without an invitation, mister, you're just
askin' for trouble. Make it good."

Blake pulled a letter from his pocket and handed it to the
redhead. "See that Colonel Howie gets this right away. It
would be proper also to let Miss Anderson have one of your
horses. Mine is too beat to pack double weight."

The cowboy studied the letter, clearly having trouble with
the words. Then he said, "Well, it's signed by the colonel
anyway, mister. You're Durant?"

"That's right. Blake Durant."

The redhead nodded. "He spoke of you. Not much, but
some."

"He doesn't know much."

Blake pushed his horse between the four. The redhead
studied him briefly, gave Lil another searching look and then
he said, "Wiles, hand over your horse. You ain't gonna see a
lady walk while you ride, are you?"

A young, pimple-faced youth scowled at the redhead but came out of the saddle. Lil smiled graciously at him. "No, I'm all right," she said, then she went on and left the others to follow. But she had only gone a few paces when the redhead galloped his horse past her, making her stop and turn her head away from the rise of dust. Coughing, Lil cursed him, her language bringing frowns to the faces of the other three cowhands. Blake put his horse into a faster walk and stayed at Lil's side. When he reached the ranch house, he swung off Sundown and tossed the reins to the pimple-faced youth.

"Just give him hay, some water and let him be. I'll unsaddle him later."

Blake went up the porch steps. He was halfway across the boards when a tall, white-haired, remarkably trim man stepped out of the house with the redhead at his side. He held Blake's letter in his hand. His cool stare went over Blake before he nodded.

"Expected you sooner, Durant," he said and extended his hand.

"I was delayed by events you should know about," Blake told him.

Then Colonel Howie saw Lil. He frowned heavily and stepped to Blake's side for a better look. Then a gleam came into his eyes. "Lil," he said.

She smiled. "Hello, Colonel. Been a long time, hasn't it?"

"Too long," he said. The colonel turned to the redhead. "It's all right, Cole. I can manage it from here."

Cole looked intently at Blake Durant and then at Lil before he waved the escorting cowboys off. When Cole had gone down the porch towards his horse, Howie said, "Come on in out of the sun, Lil. You, too, Durant. I can see you've both had a hard time."

His gaze settled on Lil's face and a thoughtful expression puckered at his brow. But he said no more until he had given them drinks in the huge living room.

"You said you were delayed, Durant. I think I'd better get the facts about that first. After that, Lil, you and I will have a private talk and see what made you change your mind about coming here. You can also tell me what breed of people marked your face."

Lil eyed him over the rim of her glass. "I'd prefer to have my position settled first, Colonel. For years I've thought about your proposal and finally decided to take you up on it. As you know, when I make up my mind on something I act immediately. Hence no fine clothes, no luggage of any kind, not even a horse to carry me."

"Later," Howie said. He sat down opposite Blake and sipped at his drink. "Well, Blake, it's been years. I confess your letter troubled me. You made no mention of your home or your family, or of Louise Yerby. Don't tell me you two didn't make a go of it?

"I won't believe that" Howie continued "because I've got some tender memories of your regard for each other, regard in fact that has spurred me to keep looking for a woman of my own. If I could even get a slight taste of that feeling for anybody, I'd be willing to smile at all the setbacks life throws at me."

Blake felt Lil's stare on him. "Louise is dead," he said. "It was an accident ... just before we were to be married. I—I'd rather not talk about it, Colonel. My brother is looking after the ranch and I'm ... well, I'm drifting ..."

"Trying to forget," said Colonel Howie, nodding his gray head in understanding. Refilling their glasses and paying no attention at all to Lil Anderson, he went on, "Now about the other business. I told you to come on out, that you were welcome at any time. But I expected you to be here a week ago."

"I got tangled up with a wagon train," Blake said.

Howie's eyes narrowed and suddenly his face was ugly. "Settlers?"

Blake nodded.

"Coming this way, Blake?"

"Yes."

Howie rose and slammed his glass down hard, breaking the stem.

He swept the rest of the glass to the floor. "How many and how close are they? By God, it was sensible of you to keep a check on them. What did you find out?"

"They're hard-working, honest people in the main, Colonel, the kind the territory needs."

"What territory, damn you, man? Are you suggesting I need settlers crowding up my country?"

Blake finished his drink and said, "Why not hear the rest of the story?"

Howie glared at him but in the face of Blake's coolness he relaxed. "All right, but make it fast. If settlers are trying to nest on my place, they'll learn it's the mistake of their lives."

Blake told about his weeks with the wagon train. Colonel Howie listened attentively. When Blake was finished he paced the room, hands locked behind his back.

Finally he stopped. "I have to see this Stanton, Blake, as soon as possible."

"He's not far off. If I've judged him right, Colonel, he won't make any mistakes this close to your territory."

"How do you figure him, Blake?" Howie asked. "All you've given me is a heap of facts, no opinion."

Lil said, "Stanton is a murdering swine, Colonel. His men did this to my face."

"And Dan Rinald? What about him?" Howie asked.

Blake shook his head. "He comes and goes, but he doesn't do much more than stir the farmers up into a fighting mood and force them to back Stanton. If you can read between the lines ..."

"Read between them I can," snorted Howie, and he resumed his pacing. "From what you've said, Stanton is not the kind of man who likes hard work. He sounds more like a dude, a cheat, a man who takes advantage of others."

"I have him pegged exactly that way," Blake admitted.

"Could Stanton and Rinald be in cahoots, Blake?"

"Well, it's something worth looking into. Are you ready to ride, Colonel?"

"Of course I'm ready to ride!" Howie stormed across the room. Then, as he drew the porch door open, Lil called out.

"What will I do, Colonel?"

"Wait," he said and went out. Blake Durant started to follow him but Lil hurried across the room and blocked his way.

"You don't want me, Blake, I know that. I know, too, that there's no way I can keep you from thinking about that—that other woman. I was a fool not to realize it was something like that in the first place."

"But I'm lucky to be the kind whose affections don't run too deep. If I can't have you, help me get the colonel. I'll do everything he asks of me. I can't go on struggling any longer. Out here I'll have no identity but what he gives me. Please, Blake, help me, please" begged Lil.

Blake Durant lifted her hand from his arm. "I think it's up to him," he muttered and went out.

Ten minutes later, Colonel Howie had his men gathered in front of the house. He told them what he wanted them to do, then warned that he didn't want bloodshed unless Stanton and his friends made trouble. If the settlers moved on and kept going, he'd be satisfied.

They were riding past the corrals when two sweat-lathered horses galloped in. There was only one rider, and he was bent across his horse's neck. Blake Durant saw a blood patch high on his shoulder. He also saw a man's body dangling across the saddle of the second horse.

Cole halted the wounded rider and Howie asked, "What happened, Bonner?"

"Settlers," Bonner, a tall gangling cowboy, said through tightly-pressed lips. His face contorted with pain.

"Where?"

Bonner straightened enough to jerk his hand behind himself.

"The canyon behind the ridge, Colonel. We were drivin' some strays when Ben got it. All I saw was three jaspers down behind the rocks. I wasn't sure if Ben was dead or not, so I dragged his horse off. I got behind them, meanin' to do what I could and they called out that they were gonna kill me and would kill any cattleman who came makin' trouble for them." Bonner shook his head. "I didn't know what the hell they were talkin' about. We ain't seen no settlers. There ain't another outfit within a hundred miles of us, is there?"

Colonel Howie muttered bitterly and swung around to face Blake. "Well, Durant, what now?"

"Three men ties up. I figure they're Dan Rinald and his two gun hands."

Howie was thoughtful for a time. "Mebbe," he grunted.

"It also ties up with what we both thought earlier about Stanton being the kind to take advantage of other people," Blake said. "He led the farming crowd out here and now he's making sure that you lock horns with them. When the damage is done he hopes to have a lot less cattlemen to worry about. I think it adds up to our getting after Rinald first."

Howie scowled. "And let them stinkin' sodbusters get a toehold in my territory?"

Blake looked thoughtfully towards the high slope Bonner had just come down.

"Colonel, they sent their message and now they'll be watching to see what move you make. When you pull out, that crowd will ride down and make more trouble. Rinald wants fight and so does Stanton, but Stanton we can handle. What we've got to do is get one of Rinald's men, Rinald himself if possible, and then we'll get to the bottom of it."

"And in the meantime do we wait here like fools?"

"No. We ride on, get into a hollow and then we send most of your hands on. When Rinald sees them on the far slopes he'll ride in or I won't ever make a decision on anything again in my life."

"Makes sense," said the redhead, Cole.

Howie glared at him and barked, "I know it does, Cole. For hell's sake, don't you start doing my thinking for me, too!" Howie squinted up the slope before he turned his horse, saying, "We'll give it a try. One try and then if it fails I'm on the warpath. Don't you try to block my way then, Durant. Don't anybody try that, ever!"

They left a man to care for Bonner and moved off. As Blake suggested, they stopped in a hollow and Cole, two other men, Howie and Blake Durant stayed put. The remainder, nineteen men, headed up the slope.

Ten minutes later the riders were out of sight. Howie drew his gun.

"Now we'll see, Blake."

He had no sooner spoken than three riders appeared behind the ranch house. Howie saw Lil come from the house, rifle in hand. When she dived down behind the trough at the side of the building and began to shoot, Howie hit his horse into a run. But Blake Durant and Cole were quicker.

CHAPTER NINE
Things That Matter

Dan Rinald and his two sidekicks, Parry Miller and Joe Elder, didn't know what hit them. Never before had they run into a fighting man as coolly calculating as Colonel Howie. Nor had they faced men trained to the perfection of Howie's hands. Without being told, Cole raced wide of the house and the other two hands went to the left, leaving the frontal attack to Howie and Blake. Before Rinald could react, Cole was in position and had the escape route to the slope cut off. The other two hands barred their progress across the clearing towards the freedom of the prairie. Colonel Howie had the front of the house covered. Moving protectively behind Lil, he opened fire. His first shot tore one of the attackers from the saddle. His second grazed the eyebrow of a man, then Cole's gun put him to the ground and he was gunless as he came to his knees. Rinald, wheeling his horse in panic, made for the prairie but ran into Blake Durant's accurate fire. When he pitched from the saddle, Blake Durant knew he'd killed him.

Colonel Howie's face was grim as he looked at the man kneeling before him. The outlaw's hands were above his head.

Lil, now that the danger was past, got to her feet, ran to the outlaw and slapped him hard across the face.

"You filthy swine, Elder!" she cried. "You held me while Rinald mauled me." Lil pushed the rifle end into Joe Elder's neck and spat in his face.

But Colonel Howie said, "Lil, killing isn't a woman's business. Stand back."

"To hell I will!" Lil looked furiously up at Howie and saw anger building in him.

Then Howie spoke, tonelessly. "Woman, while you're on my place you'll do as I say. All the time. Get back now."

Lil lowered the gun as Howie came out of the saddle. Cole Battersby dragged the second outlaw by one leg and dumped the body at Joe Elder's feet, then he turned to the colonel and said, "Want me to finish him off, Colonel? His kind have buzzards waitin' to tear 'em apart."

Howie shook his head and looked at Blake Durant. "Know him?"

Blake told him again about the attack on his camp. Howie, satisfied, said, "Well, I guess you've got the right to get the truth out of him, Blake. We'll leave you to it if you like."

Joe Elder looked up in fear as Blake grabbed his shirt. He shook his head desperately, "No, Durant, don't! I was just along for the ride. I never hurt you any."

"You tried, mister." Blake dragged him to his feet. Elder's shoulder was bleeding but otherwise he seemed unhurt. Blake swung him around and slammed him against the side of the house.

"Tell us about Mike Stanton, Elder!"

Elder shook his head again, gulping heavily, sweat running down his face in rivers.

"I don't know nothin' about Stanton."

"He visited Rinald at night, maybe three or four times in the last week, mister," Blake said.

Elder tried to squirm away but Blake held him fast against the high wall of the ranch house.

Then Colonel Howie said, "Well, he's had his say. No sense in wasting more time on him. Shoot his guts out, Blake, and leave him here. We've got other people to see."

Elder gave a sharp cry and flailed out with both hands. But Blake Durant steadied him with a jolting right to the jaw and then he shook him hard. Then he stepped back and thumbed the hammer of his gun into firing position.

"It was them," Elder sobbed. "It was the others and Stanton."

"Did Stanton make his plans with Rinald?"

"Yes."

"Back in Lusc?"

"Before that. We ran into Stanton and his crowd in Cheyenne. Dan knew Stanton from way back.

Stanton had a plan to take this valley and Dan threw in with him. I figured it was loco from the start, worryin' them farmers into a fighting mood, but Dan and Stanton said to do it. Then yesterday Stanton rode out, saw us and said we should make trouble here. Hell, we figured that was loco, Parry and me, there against a big outfit like this. But what could we do? It was buck Dan or take our chances with you."

Colonel Howie turned to Lil. "Go into the house and stay there, woman." He swung into the saddle and motioned for Cole Battersby to fetch Elder's horse. "Get up," he said. When the hellion was in the saddle, Howie said, "Time we paid some new settlers a call, Durant. When we get there, Elder, I want you to point out these thievin' scum, Stanton and his helpers. That's all I want you to do. Do you hear me?"

Blake was on Sundown when he said, "I don't think we'll have to wait for talk, Colonel. As soon as Stanton sees Elder, he'll know the game is up. I'd like it, though, if you told your men to go easy with the farmers. You have my guarantee that they want no part of a range war."

"Want it or not, they've bought in, Blake. What the hell do you think I am? You figure I should let them settle, make trouble for me, steal my beef, unsettle my men?"

"Meet them before you decide what to do with them, Colonel. You used to be a man who compromised."

"Used to be," Howie snorted. "That was before I learned a man who trusts anybody is a damned fool. People are all out for what they can get, any way they can get it."

Blake Durant said no more. Riding beside the white-haired army man, he watched him closely. He had little doubt that most of Howie's gruffness was a front to hide a generous nature. He knew Howie too well to believe differently. A few miles farther on, they linked up with the other hands and, close-bunched, took Joe Elder towards the showdown.

* * *

"Oh, Pa, it *is* beautiful!" Ellen Farner cried out. "I've never seen anything like it before. Just look at the river, so clean and sparkling. And the grass is greener than any I've ever seen! No man can keep all this for himself."

Roland Farner nodded. He was looking at the finest valley he had ever seen. Already he could visualize homes, a general store to serve their needs, and a community house everybody could draw on in times of want. He could see people walking lazily in the main street.

"You're right, girl," he said, "it is a place for everybody. We'll make our home here."

Ellen leaned across the wagon seat and kissed him tenderly. Then she hugged his arm against her bosom and with bright-eyed excitement looked back to see the other farmers standing beside their wagons. The beauty of the valley was in them. They had finally found a home.

Farner worked his wagon in against the bank of the creek as Mike Stanton rode up. Stanton looked sober. He ignored Ellen and said:

"I want the wagons put in a circle, Farner. I want everything in order in case of an attack."

"From Dan Rinald?" Farner asked.

"Maybe. But my worst worry is Colonel Howie. No man would give up this kind of country without a fight, and it's already common knowledge that Howie will let no settler, man or woman, come within twenty miles of him. I said to set a tight circle and don't argue with me."

Mike Stanton rode off and Ellen said, "I think he's wrong, Pa. None of us has met Colonel Howie yet. How can any of us say what he will or won't do? He might welcome settlers. He might *want* neighbors."

"He might, Ellen," Farner said. "But until we know for sure, we'd better let Stanton have his way. Just as soon as things are organized here, I'm riding on. I want to see Howie myself and talk to him."

"Can I come, Pa?"

Farner shook his head. "No, Ellen, this is something I have to do on my own. I have to take full responsibility. If Howie is a butcher and a land-crazy fool, then I'll suffer and the rest of you will have due warning."

Ellen opened her mouth to argue but Farner waved a hand for her to be silent. "I've made up my mind, Ellen. Don't worry me about it again. Just do as you're told."

Ellen Farner looked slightly peeved for a moment, but then she let her gaze sweep again over the rich, fertile country. Like her father, she had already staked a claim to part of the valley.

Later in the afternoon, when she walked along the creek bank on her own, still trying to sort out her thoughts, she saw a line of riders bearing down from the high slope beyond the creek. Obviously these men didn't belong to the wagon train. Who were they? she asked herself.

She moved into the shade of tall cottonwoods and waited for the riders to come closer. Suddenly she was aware that they were riding in file, much the same as cavalry soldiers she'd seen on parade days. Could the army be this far out in the wilderness? Then the truth of it struck Ellen. Colonel Howie, the man Mike Stanton claimed had full control of this country, had been a cavalry officer. These were his men! Ellen felt a tightness rise inside her. She looked anxiously behind her but the camp was a quarter mile away and she knew she couldn't hope to make it across the open country without being seen.

Nevertheless she had decided to make a run for it when she sighted Blake Durant on his huge black stallion. At the same moment Blake Durant saw her, and immediately he broke away from the riders and came thundering down towards her.

Durant drew rein in the shadows. "Where is your father, Miss Farner?"

"At the camp, Mr. Durant. Who are those men and what are you doing with them?"

"I haven't got time to explain." He paused. "Can you trust me?"

Ellen's gaze studied his face. She knew she could never actually defy this stranger who kept coming into her life, who was always on hand just prior to trouble starting. Although she couldn't quite make up her mind about him, she was impressed by the fact that he was helping others all the time.

"Trust you?" she said. "What is it you want me to do?"

Blake told her about Rinald's attack on the Howie ranch house and of the capture of Joe Elder. Then he said, "Go find your father and tell him to draw the farmers back. We want no fight with them."

"We?" Ellen asked, studying the riders who had reined up nearby and were bunched behind a white-haired, grave faced man with piercing gray-blue eyes and a tight-lipped mouth. Ellen could feel the power in this man; he had authority, strength. She knew at once that he was Colonel Howie, who Mike Stanton had warned them often about. But the idea of Stanton tricking the farmers into fighting Howie was almost too much for Ellen to believe.

Blake said, "Colonel Howie hired me to work for him. The rest will have to wait for the moment. But I do know that Stanton aims to use all of you to get what he wants, so find your father and make him draw back his men. If he stands and fights, he can't win. Colonel Howie's men are seasoned fighters and they back him to a man."

Ellen licked at her lips. She couldn't take her eyes off this man, and she felt as if he must hear the pounding of her heart.

"I'll tell him," she said suddenly.

He smiled and touched her arm. "Hurry, Ellen."

Blake Durant drew back. Ellen turned and walked quickly away, heading for her father's wagon. Minutes later, as she spoke to her father, Colonel Howie and Blake Durant led the twenty men to the wagon camp clearing.

Rick Trice was the first to sight them. He gave an immediate alarm and then Tom Legarde and Sel Watson appeared, rifles at the ready.

"No!" Farner cried. "Don't shoot!"

The men gathered at Farner's wagon and watched in silence as the line of riders spread out across the clearing and began to circle Mike Stanton's wagon.

Then Stanton came running down the timbered slope.

He stopped just as Jute Carney and Jimmy Blunt appeared at the side of his wagon. For a moment it looked as though Stanton was going to come on, but then, backing off, he disappeared in the pines.

Colonel Howie addressed Carney and Blunt. "I'm looking for a man named Stanton who hired this scum, Joe Elder, to make trouble at my spread. Fetch him."

Jute Carney's face went dark with anger. "Who the hell are you? What the blazes do you think you're doing here?"

"I'm Colonel Howie and I own all the land in this valley. Do you work for Stanton?"

Jute Carney's lips peeled back in a snarl. "Sure I work for him. And this is his country—he's staked his claim."

Howie leaned forward in the saddle, his eyes blazing. "I own this country. I've said it twice now and I don't mean to repeat myself again. One of you go fetch Stanton and we'll have this out. That way nobody will get hurt unless he openly asks for trouble."

Jimmy Blunt said, "Go get him, Jute."

Carney's hard gaze slashed at Blunt. "What for, Jimmy? Hell, are we gonna let these jaspers ride in and start throwing their weight about? This is Stanton land as far as I'm concerned, and—"

"Get Stanton!" Howie roared.

Jute Carney, stepping two paces away from Blunt, snarled, "Find him yourself, Howie." Then Carney drew his gun and fired.

The bullet whistled over Howie's head. Before Blunt could draw to support Carney's move, Cole Battersby's Peacemaker roared. Jute Carney, ready to trigger again, threw out his hands and his gun went flying. Shot through the heart, Carney did a crazy little dance and fell on his face, dead.

Jimmy Blunt grunted a curse as he saw the guns of Howie's men leveled on him. His lips peeled back and he snapped, "Seems you got what you wanted out here, Durant. What happens to me?"

"You'll get a fair trial, Blunt. I don't think you killed anybody in cold blood; that's not in you as I've seen it. But you worked for a man who butchered a lot of people and who schemed to have a lot more butchered. Did you know what was going on?"

Blunt nodded, his face set hard.

"Then you're under arrest, Blunt. Colonel Howie is the law in these parts so you'll have to answer to him for everything you and Stanton have done."

Jimmy Blunt smiled thinly. "You won't see me beggin'. I came into this with my eyes wide open. I backed Stanton all the way."

"You weren't as brutal as Schofield or Carney, Blunt. That might weigh up in your favor."

Blunt gave a crooked smile. "Don't sweet-talk me, Durant. I owe you something for the beating you gave me. I owe you, too, for all the trouble you've caused us. Without you, Stanton would have pulled this off and we'd have taken over Howie's empire. As it is ..."

Jimmy Blunt shrugged and moved back to the wagon's side. He stood there, his face tight, his eyes defiant.

Then he said, "I'm daring you to draw against me, Durant."

Howie said, "The man has guts, Durant, no matter how much his mind is twisted. But you've got no reason to call him."

"No reason not to," Blake said, then he moved Sundown out of the ranks and climbed down.

The two men faced each other. Suddenly Blunt dipped his shoulder. His hand hit the butt of his gun and the hand rose. But Blake's move was a blur of motion. Blunt's Colt was still coming up when Blake shot him through the neck. Blunt fell back against the wagon, blood spurting from his throat.

Blake said, "It could have been different."

Blunt lifted his gun, determination bright in his eyes.

"Finish it, Durant!" Howie shouted.

Blake's shot almost drowned the colonel's words. Blunt's body buckled under the impact of the slug. His gun dropped from his fingers. As he was going down, he swore. Then he hit the ground and lay still.

Blake Durant was walking towards Blunt's body when he sighted Stanton running up the slope towards the thicker timber on the rise. He drew Howie's attention to him and Cole Battersby and five others immediately broke away from Howie's side and put their mounts into a gallop. Mike Stanton, in full view of everyone, broke to the right, then the left, slipped and fell and scrambled to his feet. In blind panic he ran into trees and tripped over brush.

Cole Battersby and his companions spread put and thundered up after him. Stanton, finally trapped, halted and glared furiously at them, hand over his gun butt. But as they came on, his courage broke and he lifted his hands high above his head.

"You're going to hang, Stanton," Cole said.

Mike Stanton's face went to chalk. He watched the others closing in and then he saw Roland Farner and his friends coming in a group up the hill. He knew then that he had no chance. He dropped his hands and went into a crouch. Cole Battersby put three bullets into him before Mike Stanton fell and lay still, his shirt stained with blood, his face buried in the dirt he had hoped to own.

* * *

Blake Durant was standing on the porch looking into the distance when Howie made his final summing up. "So, Farner, the way I see it, you people have come a long way. On Durant's say-so, you haven't made any trouble of your own, but you got caught up in somebody else's. I've thought about your position and I've discussed the situation with my men. None of us sees you as a risk to the peace out here, so I'm going to let you have that valley. But, by hell —and I mean this—if one single cow of mine is butchered without my permission, or if there is any act at all which breaks the rules I have laid down, then I'll come in force and drive you off. Make your own community and run it honestly. That way we'll get on fine."

Blake stepped down from the porch and made his way to the barn where he saddled Sundown. From the moment he'd decided to pay Colonel Howie a call, he'd looked forward to the loneliness of the wild country, space where he could lose himself ... and perhaps forget.

Now he felt the world closing in on him again. Lil Anderson was staying. How close Howie would let her get to him was a matter for the two of them and nobody else. Lil had already changed a great deal. She seemed to be under the spell of Colonel Howie.

Blake swung onto Sundown and was coming out of the barn when Ellen Farner appeared in the doorway. There were tears in her eyes when she saw his saddle roll. "You're going, Mr. Durant?"

"I feel I must, Ellen."

"But why? We've apologized for our behavior. Blake, I—I can't let you ride off like this."

Blake said, "Ellen, you're a fine woman and you're facing a wonderful future. In time you'll have a town that will prosper. But I can't play any part in it."

"Why not, Blake? Why?"

Blake Durant looked past her, into the distance. His eyes clouded. "Because it's not time yet, Ellen. Some day it might be."

Ellen brightened a little and moved closer. "When, Blake? I can wait. Father told me not to say anything like this. He seems to think—"

"Your father is a wise man, Ellen." Blake leaned from the saddle and kissed her. When he straightened, her eyes were bright.

"Oh, Blake, please come back! Please!"

Blake heeled Sundown away. He didn't look back. Before him was open country. There would be new towns, new people, new experiences. Perhaps, one day, he would ride back here, one day when the past was blurred in his memory. Then, if Ellen Farner was still here and still wanted him ... then, perhaps...

www.ingramcontent.com/pod-product-compliance
Lightning Source LLC
Chambersburg PA
CBHW060939050726

47592CB00003B/1018